ANASAZI INTRIGUE

The Adventures of John and Julia Evans

By Linda Weaver Clarke

Copyright © Linda Weaver Clarke, 2010. Second Edition, 2012.
All rights reserved. No part of this book may be reproduced or
transmitted in any form without permission in writing from the author.
Recording of this work for the handicapped is permitted.

Red Mountain Shadows Publishing
Cover Design by George Amos Clarke
Printed in the United States of America on acid-free paper.

Anasazi Intrigue: The Adventures of John and Julia Evans
By Linda Weaver Clarke
www.lindaweaverclarke.com

ISBN-13: 978-1481266864
ISBN-10: 1481266861

Names, characters, places, and incidents are the product of the author's
imagination, and any resemblance to actual persons, living or dead, events,
or locales is purely coincidental.

ALSO BY LINDA WEAVER CLARKE

Romantic Cozy Mysteries
The Bali Mystery
The Shamrock Case
The Missing Heir
The Mysterious Doll
Her Lost Love
Mystery on the Bayou
The Lighthouse Secret

Mystery/Suspense
Anasazi Intrigue
Mayan Intrigue
Montezuma Intrigue
Desert Intrigue

Historical Adventure Romance
The Rebels of Cordovia
The Highwayman of Cordovia
The Fox of Cordovia

Historical Romances
Melinda and the Wild West

Edith and the Mysterious Stranger
Jenny's Dream
Sarah's Special Gift
Elena, Woman of Courage

Other Books
Bedtime Stories: Shadows In My Room
Reflections of the Heart
Searching for True Happiness

Dedication

I dedicate this book to my sweet and supportive husband, George Amos Clarke. He encouraged me from the beginning, created my website, and lifted my spirits when I got discouraged. He told me that he had faith in me. I couldn't have asked for a more devoted and loving husband. Thank you, Sweetheart.

Preface

The television mystery series *Hart to Hart* was the inspiration for this story. It featured a married couple investigating and solving crimes. The couple was madly in love. You laughed at the humor and sighed at the romance. The Adventures of John and Julia Evans has great values along with a little suspense and adventure. Add a couple of teenagers and a grown daughter, and you have quite a mixture. Julia is a reporter for a daily newspaper, and John is a professional knife maker. Because of her curiosity and wanting to get a good story, Julia gets herself into a bunch of trouble. Before long, she finds herself and her husband up to their necks in danger and running for their lives.

Chapter 1

A thunderous crash could be heard in the distance as a home collapsed and crumbled into the rushing waters below. Several people were standing at the edge of a hilltop in Santa Clara, Utah, watching their valley being destroyed before their very eyes.

When Julia Roberts Evans saw the home fall into the depths of the water, she gasped. She put her hand lightly against her mouth with sorrow. John instantly wrapped his arm around his wife's waist and pulled her close.

Standing on the hill and watching the destruction below was an emotional experience for Julia as she nestled into her husband's arm. She was a reporter and was supposed to write about the tragedy, but this was personal. Her valley and her friends' homes were being ripped apart. The destruction below wrenched at Julia's heart. Her home was safe and she had lost nothing, but her heart went out to the family who had just lost their home and property.

The torrent had eaten away the dirt of the riverbank and the foundation of the house. With no support, the home fell into the rapidly flowing river and was swept away downstream. The trees and shrubs that once lined the small five-foot-wide river were now gone, uprooted and swept away by the violent and turbulent flow of water. What took years for nature to create, nature was able to destroy within seconds. Who would ever have guessed that the creek would swell to such width, viciously cutting away at the landscape?

Julia and her husband had moved here twenty-one years ago. Her children were born and raised here. She had taken them to the small river below and had floated little wooden boats downstream. They had gone wading; even her husband had slipped off his shoes and joined them. After a few days of 110-degree temperatures, they had driven to this spot and splashed one another with cool water.

Now this once tranquil stream, which could easily be crossed on foot or in a car, was now as wide as the length of a football field, and it was taking everything within its path. The speed of the river had once been five cubic feet per second, and now it was more than 6,500 cubic feet per second. In three days time, it had dug into the earth's surface, carving away at the banks and creating ridges as high as thirty to forty feet. The torrent was digging at the earth at ten feet per hour like a plow and sweeping the red dirt down the river into Arizona and Nevada.

John shook his head in dismay as he combed his fingers through his wavy, dark brown hair. "I just helped someone move their stuff into a neighbor's garage yesterday."

"Oh?" said Julia. "That's good."

"No," he said with regret. "This morning, we had to hurry and take the stuff out. The river had eaten away so much during the night that the neighbor's home was in danger. We just barely made it, Julia."

John was one of the volunteers who had worked feverishly

to help the residents remove what they could from the homes that were threatened by the river, but there were those who escaped with only the clothes on their backs. About two hundred homes were damaged and twenty-five were completely destroyed. With the help of the community and religious leaders, homes were found for the homeless.

Julia turned to her husband and said with concern, "Why is the flooding so bad this year?"

"Six weeks of rain following a seven-year drought is the main reason," said John as he motioned toward the river. "Built-up debris blocked the river channel and the only direction to go was outward, toward farmland and homes. Not only that, the heavy snow in the mountains seemed to be a blessing to our desert land, but the unusually warm January has melted the snow too fast."

Julia shook her head. "Way too fast!"

"Yup! Add that with the constant rain, and the saturated ground couldn't hold any more. So far, the estimated damage is nearly two hundred million dollars. Anyway, that's what the fire department figured."

He looked down at Julia with his rich chocolate-brown eyes and a grim look on his face. His eyes and countenance had softened through the years, along with having three daughters to raise. If daughters couldn't soften a man, then nothing would.

John's square jaw was set as he pushed his fingers through his hair once again. "Well, all the sandbags we put out along the river didn't help much. They were washed down the river as well."

"I noticed." Julia turned to her husband and said, "Personally, I think this assignment is a little too close for comfort. It's been an emotional roller coaster for me, and I'm supposed to be a professional. I should report without emotions."

She shook her head in discouragement.

John stared at her with arched brows, rubbing his chin thoughtfully. "Hmm, a non-emotional reporter ... so reporters aren't supposed to have feelings when they report about their neighbor's home crushing into the depths below? Reporters aren't supposed to be full of empathy when a person ends up homeless?" He shook his head and narrowed his eyes, "Julia, I believe you're in the wrong profession."

She gave a hint of smile as she said, "Yeah, you've got a point there. Just tell that to Ted, my coworker. He says that professional reporters aren't supposed to get emotionally involved. Our duty is to report and nothing else."

"He's a lying sack of..."

John quickly stopped his thoughts when Julia gave him a stern look, and he instantly changed his mind. She was always getting after him for saying a few choice words when he would hit his finger with a hammer or when the computer would not obey his command. He needed to work on that.

John grinned guiltily and said, "What I meant to say is that he's a lying sack of manure, Julia."

She smiled knowingly and nodded her head. As she began taking a few pictures of the disaster below, she had an uneasy feeling as if she was being watched. She lowered her camera and looked around. Then their eyes met.

A tall man dressed in a white jacket and white baggy pants was standing a short distance away, watching her intently. She wondered if her imagination was getting away with her because he looked at least six-feet-five inches tall. He had broad shoulders and shoulder-length hair that was pulled into a ponytail. A chill went down her spine and a sense of foreboding spread over her.

The stranger grinned and commented nonchalantly, "Aren't you that reporter, Julia Evans? I've seen your byline and photo in the paper and read a few of your articles. They're good."

Feeling awkward, Julia gave a nod. "Thank you."

"I'm new in town and haven't read a small town newspaper like this before. It's very interesting, indeed, with a homey touch."

The stranger dropped a cigarette to the ground and smashed it with the toe of his shoe. He grinned, as his piercing blue eyes swept over her with great interest.

Feeling uncomfortable, she turned toward her husband and slipped her hand into the crook of his arm. Why was he staring at her like that? It was disconcerting, but deep inside she seemed to know that their paths would cross once again. The thought of it sent a shiver up her spine.

"You okay, Sweetheart? Are you cold?" asked John with concern.

"No." Julia shook her head and tugged at her husband's arm nervously. "Let's drive to green Valley and see the damage over there. I heard it was hit the hardest."

Julia needed more pictures, but the main reason for leaving was the discomfort she felt in the presence of the man in white. She needed to leave. There was something about him that was disturbing but she did not understand why.

As Julia walked toward the car, she still felt his eyes upon her. Without hesitation, she quickly opened the door and slid in. As they pulled away from the curb, she turned and saw the man in white watching them drive away.

As he drove, John looked over at Julia and saw the soberness on her face. He knew this was a tough assignment, simply because it hit home. And to not be emotionally involved would be impossible. Ted was a complete jerk, not to mention insensitive, proud, and overbearing.

"Are you still having those dreams?" asked John.

Julia nodded. "It's so strange. I can't figure it out. I find myself admiring this beautiful pendant. I can tell it's from another time … an ancient artifact." She hesitated for a moment, biting her lip nervously as she looked at John. "But there's more I haven't told you."

John could see that she was uneasy about the dream, so he encouraged her to continue. "Hmmm, you've got my attention, M'darlin'. Tell me about it."

"Well, after admiring it, I snatch it up, stuff it in my pocket, and then take off running."

"You're a thief?" John said teasingly. "Why didn't you tell me that part of your dream?"

"Well, I was embarrassed. Why would I steal something of great value when it's completely against my nature?"

"If I didn't know you so well, I would laugh and tell you to go out and buy one. Then all your dreams would go away."

Julia stared out the window, wondering why she had been dreaming of stealing a valuable artifact.

When John saw the concerned look on her face, he added softly, "You know I believe in your dreams, Julia. I wouldn't ignore it. Your dreams are always significant. It'll come to you eventually." He raised his brow. "So what does this coveted pendant look like, anyway?"

"Coveted?" Julia punched his arm. "That's not funny!"

"Hey! Maybe it's your secret desire, to have something from the ancient past," John said with a chuckle.

Julia frowned.

"Sorry," he said, trying to suppress a smile and not succeeding very well.

"And wipe that silly grin off your face, too!"

John hastily clapped his hand over his mouth.

Noticing his playfulness, she said, "Take your hand away. I know you're still smiling."

He removed his hand and sure enough, his grin was wider than ever. "But I can't help it, Julia. The thought of you becoming a thief is so outrageous. You're a person who loves to visit museums and admire the past. You wouldn't steal."

"That's the part that bothers me, Honey," she said mournfully.

Knowing she was feeling distraught over the dream, he stopped playing around and softly asked, "Can you remember what it looks like?"

Julia nodded. "The only thing I remember is that it's a red triangle pendant. I have a feeling that it's very special for some reason, and I'm not sure why."

Seeing her somber look, he said softly, "Don't worry. It'll come to you, Sweetheart."

As they rode to Green Valley, they saw the remains of eighteen homes that were destroyed, which had been at the mercy of the raging river.

"John! Pull over here!" Julia said with urgency. "I need to get out."

He immediately pulled the car over, and Julia hopped out with her camera in hand. What she saw was a threshold standing alone. The door was wide open and swinging on its hinges. The home was gone. It had sunk into the depths of the river and left behind its threshold. What a sight! Part of a fence was hanging over the edge of the thirty-foot-high bank, and a few shrubs were dangling by their roots.

Lost homes could be replaced, but the sad thing about this flood was the loss of irreplaceable and precious treasures that had no value to anyone but the owner, such as pictures and memories of the past.

John slowly walked toward Julia, amazed at the sight before him.

After snapping a few photos, Julia looked up at him and said, "Now let's go to the north end of Gunlock."

"Aren't the bridges washed out?"

"That's right, so we'll have to go around it."

"I understand that a helicopter is taking food to the residents until the bridges are repaired."

She nodded. This flood had affected the whole community.

It was a thirty-minute drive to the nonexistent bridge. John pulled over to the side, and they hopped out. As his wife snapped a few pictures, John investigated the remains of the destroyed bridge.

Seeing an extra lush area in the distance, Julia became curious. The desert seemed to be greener than usual from all the rain. She walked toward it and found a small pond surrounded by shrubs and bushes. What a pleasant sight! Apparently, this remote and secluded area wasn't flooded for some reason, probably because it was away from the main river and protected by the hills surrounding it. It looked untouched and serene, being fed by streams from the mountains above. As she inspected it, she found about three-dozen fish in the pond, floating lifelessly.

Feeling a little puzzled, she yelled, "John! Come here."

He saw her in the distance and sauntered towards her. "What's up?"

"This."

She pointed to the pond.

John knelt down on the grassy bank and inspected the fish closely. "Now what do you suppose happened here?"

"That's why I called you over. There's so many. If there were just one or two, then I wouldn't question it, but three dozen? It couldn't be a coincidence. What do you think?"

"I wouldn't think so, either."

"Where did they come from?"

John shook his head with a puzzled look. "I'd figure these fish must have come from streams above us or below us."

"Below us?" Julia questioned.

"Yup. Either they swam upstream from Gunlock reservoir or they came downstream from Baker's Dam."

Julia immediately turned on her heels and headed for the car.

"Where are you going?"

She turned around and looked over her shoulder. "I'm going to get a gunnysack and take the fish to Matthew at Dixie State College. He's a good chemist and will be able to tell us what happened to them."

John nodded his approval. "Not a bad idea. Why are you so curious?"

Julia grinned from ear to ear. "Now, my darling husband, have you ever run into a reporter who wasn't curious?"

"Hmmm, I don't believe I have, Julia."

John chuckled as he watched her walk towards the car. Julia was a determined woman with rich auburn hair that barely touched the tops of her shoulders. She had expressive hazel eyes with gold and green flecks and long dark eyelashes. She had a genuine smile and a deep belief and faith in God.

As John watched her walk gracefully away, he could not help but think how stunningly beautiful she was. She had such grace and poise, even in her Levis and red cotton ribbed tee shirt. He loved everything about her, even her stubborn ways. She was so daring that it scared the bee-gee-bees out of him. She was completely opposite from him, which made his life with Julia even more interesting. He could never figure out what made her so strong willed.

John was a gentle man with a great sense of humor and teasing ways. He was more cautious and guarded, not one to take chances. At the same time, he was more subdued and quiet. He was laid back and took life as it came. He also tried to make sure there was a certain spark in his relationship with Julia by spending time with her and paying attention to her needs. Sometimes he would forget those needs, simply because of the stress at work. He tried not to neglect his wife. He knew it was not right to allow a marriage to deteriorate simply because of neglect such as working late on a project or taking off with his archaeologist friend. He had to remember that she was a very important part of his life and could not take her for granted. They did have a few things in common, though, and that was their love for music. They both loved jazz and the blues.

Julia was a newspaper reporter for the *Dixie Chronicle*. She wrote editorial columns on newsworthy subjects such as the famous St. George Rodeo or the grand outdoor Arts Festival during Easter time. Now she was assigned to cover the flood caused from the Santa Clara/Virgin Rivers.

Just before her birthday last year, her friends told her that women tended to get depressed when turning forty. But it wasn't so with Julia. She felt it was a new beginning. All her children were now independent. Since she had more time on her hands, she decided it was about time to work a little harder so she could get a promotion. Her goal was to get the "assignment of a lifetime" before she turned forty-one.

Julia returned in no time with a gunnysack dangling from her hand. She stooped down next to the bank and began scooping up a few fish with her hands, placing them in the gunnysack while John watched contentedly.

At the age of forty-two, John was a master knife and sword maker. Tempering steel into creative shapes and styles brought him great joy. He was unusually tall with broad shoulders and a strong jaw. His bulging biceps came from lifting and working with large pieces of steel. His mother often told him that he had inherited his dark brown eyes, olive complexion, and rugged build from her side of the family. She had named him after his grandfather, John Roberts. That knowledge made him feel proud, knowing he had come from a great heritage.

John sat down on a boulder and watched intently as Julia gracefully bent over the bank and scooped a fish into the sack. This woman before him was determined to find out why these fish were dead and no one could sway her decision. How he admired her tenacity!

After years of marriage, she still intrigued him. He had read that once a man stopped watching his wife as she moved about and stopped noticing her shapely curves, then something was definitely wrong with their relationship. Soon Julia would be forty-one, and she looked more appealing to him than the first day of their marriage

As Julia worked, a water snake slithered near the bank and startled her. She gasped and jumped aside, but after realizing what it was, she sighed with relief and just gave it a little push with her fingertips so it would head in the opposite direction.

"Go away! I don't need your help," she said patiently.

The snake slithered toward the nearby rocks and disappeared out of sight. John chuckled. She wasn't afraid of anything.

He leaned his forearms against his knees and said, "You know what, Julia?"

She turned and saw him grinning from ear to ear. "What?"

"I'm sure glad you're not like the typical woman, afraid of creeping things."

Julia narrowed her eyes. "Is that a compliment or what?"

He chuckled. "A compliment, of course! You're not one of those squeamish women who squeal with a high-pitched voice at the sight of a snake, and you don't mind touching slimy fish."

Julia laughed. "And why do you think that's so great?"

He thought for a moment and then smiled. "'Cause you'd make me do it, I guess. I'd rather not."

Julia shook her head with amusement. "On the farm, we had plenty of these garden snakes. Once my brother found a nest of them near the house, and I remember how he would pick one up and try to scare me with it, but I wasn't afraid. He wasn't going to get the best of me. Besides, it's no big deal. They aren't venomous."

John grinned. "That's a tongue twister. Do you think you can say it three times?"

She stared at him, seeing the challenge in his eyes, but shook her head. "No, thanks. You try it."

John concentrated for a few moments and repeated, "Venomous, venomous, venomous."

"Wow!" Julia laughed. "I'm impressed."

He grinned mischievously. "It's all in the tongue and lips."

"Really?"

"Uh-huh."

Julia smiled with a teasing glint in her eyes and said, "So, you accuse women of being afraid of reptiles. How about you? Are you squeamish when it comes to snakes?"

John looked offended. "Are you kidding? Of course not!" Then he smiled. "I can't stand the slimy creatures personally, and I wouldn't have pushed it away with my hand as you did, but I wouldn't jump around frantically screaming."

Julia laughed. "What would you have done?"

"Now that's easy to answer. I would have gotten a stick and slid it under him and dropped him in the water. That's the safe way to do it."

Julia smiled at his answer. "How about dead fish?"

"If you wanted me to put them in the sack for you, I'd do it, all right. Personally, though, I prefer watching you do it."

"Watching? Now that's the lazy man in you, I do say."

"No, I'm smart. You see, I get to sit here and watch an attractive woman. And you look pretty darn good from this angle."

Julia suppressed a smile. "Pshaw! You're just flirting with your wife and trying to hide the fact that you're squeamish. I bet you anything that you would squirm if you had to pick up a water snake with your hand and not a stick."

John lifted his brow at her challenge. He immediately hopped up and walked toward her. He stooped down beside her and looked into her large hazel eyes. He saw the challenge in them, and she was grinning from ear to ear.

With mischief lacing his eyes, he said, "Squirm, you say?"

Julia nodded curtly. "I dare you to look for that water snake and pick it up." With more emphasis, she repeated, "I *dare* you."

He chuckled at her playfulness. "I'll show you squirm!"

John took her by the shoulders, pulled her close to him, and kissed her soundly on the lips. Then he spread gentle whispering kisses down her neck, nibbling as he went. It did not take long for her to giggle and begin to squirm. The goose bumps that he was causing spread down her arms and up her spine.

Julia gave one powerful shove and said, "Stop it! You're distracting me."

"More like squirm, if you ask me."

Suppressing a smile, she got to her feet and said, "You're just trying to change the subject so you don't have to take my challenge."

"Your challenge?" he said as he stood.

She pointed toward the rocky area. "The water snake went that-a-way, Mister."

"Hey! I'm not interested in any dad-blame snake. I'm having too much fun."

Julia rolled her eyes. "Sorry, but I've got to get these fish to Matthew before he leaves the lab."

John couldn't help but grin as he asked lightheartedly, "Hey, Julia, are you sure you want to leave now? I was just getting started."

She gazed at the unusually lush green area. "You always choose the most romantic places, don't you?"

"Of course. Look around us," he said with a wave of his hand. "We have slithering snakes for an audience and dead slimy fish to scent up the atmosphere." He took a deep exaggerated breath and let it out. "Ah! What an aroma!"

Julia giggled at his sense of humor, giving him a coy smile. And with that, he grabbed her into his arms and began spreading a whisper of warm kisses down her cheek and across her jaw line. Then lifting her chin with his finger, he pressed his lips to hers, giving her the message of undying love. As he enfolded her in his arms and gently caressed her back, he gave her a kiss that turned her mind to mush, made her melt into his arms, and sent a tingle of warmth from her lips right down to her toes.

John adored his wife and companion. This woman gave meaning to his life, made him want to strive to be better. Not only that, she made him feel like a man, and the effect she had on him was indescribable!

When John heard her sigh, he released Julia's lips and asked, "Do you still want to get these fish to Matthew?"

Julia smiled as her eyes flickered open. "What fish?"

Linda Weaver Clarke

Chapter 2

Ivins was known as the "Home of the Red Mountain," surrounded by desert land, cactus, silvery-leafed sagebrush, and creosote bushes here and there. It was a wild land, uncultivated but beautiful in its own right. In the distance was a range of coral-red mountains, standing majestically to the north.

It had been over two weeks, and Julia was still waiting to hear from Matthew about the dead fish. She and her husband were standing at the top of a hill near the Anasazi petroglyphs in Ivins, looking down at the Santa Clara River. Julia's boss wanted her to take some photos and report about the "aftermath" of the flood.

John very seldom had time alone with Julia and was grateful for the short but valuable time he had with her after work. It was so nice to be out this afternoon and be able to converse and be together.

As they gazed at the river, they noticed that it had calmed down quite a bit. The giant cottonwood trees that had once lined the sides of this peaceful creek had been uprooted and washed downstream. The land below seemed bare and desolate without the trees and shrubbery.

When Julia's cell phone rang, John meandered over to a

boulder and sat in front of some Anasazi artwork.

"Hello, Bill! What's up?" She paused. "Oh, no! That's awful." The sadness in Julia's expression was obvious, but it instantly changed to wonderment. "Why, that's a miracle. I can't believe it. Thanks for calling. I'll see you later."

John looked over his shoulder with curiosity and asked, "What was that all about?"

"My boss was telling me about an elderly woman who grabbed what she could with the help of her neighbors but wasn't able to get everything. She lost her husband's and her own Book of Remembrance, which had pictures of their family, their ancestors, and their biographies."

"Man, that's tough. You can't replace pictures."

"That's right." Julia stashed her phone in her camera bag. "All those memories were swept away in the flood. Then the following day after her home was gone, a knock came at the door where she was staying. And lo and behold, a man was standing there with the book in his hand. He said that he found it washed up on a tree stump near his home. Needless to say, she wept for joy."

"Wow!"

"But that's not all. The following day, her husband's book was found."

"Now that's a double miracle, I'd say."

"It certainly is. She said the kindness of others has been overwhelming."

Julia knew that stories of hope, charity, and little miracles seem to uplift others and have a wonderful effect on people during a crisis such as this. These stories needed to be told.

She believed in miracles, and this story was one that brightened the day for her, one that she needed to hear.

She had felt a little down lately because of a certain annoying coworker, but this lifted her spirits.

Julia pulled her camera out, turned back to the river below, and began taking a few pictures while John turned his attention to the ever-intriguing petroglyphs of the Anasazi Indians.

As he stared at the Anasazi artwork, rubbing his chin with his hand, he commented, "You know, Julia, this looks just like two long-horned mountain sheep. Man, rock art is so fascinating. Did you know they have located two hundred and twenty-five Anasazi sites in Utah, Arizona, Colorado, Nevada, and New Mexico?"

"That's sure a lot."

"Yup. When I came here six months ago to watch the archaeologists dig, they told me the Anasazi might be the ancestors of the Pueblo Indians." He paused, staring at the rock art. "Here's a hump-backed man playing a flute. He's called a Kokopelli."

"Kokopelli?"

"Yeah. He represents fertility, prosperity, and celebration. Interesting! And look at this, Julia."

She had been taking a few pictures while listening to John and turned to see what he was pointing at. "What's that?"

"It's a spiral."

She laughed. "I can see that. Do you know what it means?"

"Yup, I sure do. It's the symbol of life and death, man's journey through life while seeking his spiritual center." He turned around and saw her standing on top of a large flat boulder near the edge of the hill. "Be careful. You're a little too close for comfort, my Dear. I don't want your 'spiral of life' coming to an end prematurely. You're making me real nervous."

She smiled and stepped back. "I just need a few more shots. It's sure beautiful up here, John."

He nodded. It was just like her to stand so close and admire the beauties below. How he wished she wouldn't do that!

Julia looked at the Indian art in front of John and asked, "So, do the archaeologists find out what the people are like just by examining their artwork?"

"That's right. All these clues are like a large jigsaw puzzle. I learned that they settled here about 200 AD and disappeared around the year 1200."

Julia hung her camera over her shoulder and folded her arms across her waist as she listened.

"Why do you suppose they left, Julia?"

"Perhaps a drought forced them to leave."

He shrugged. "Could be, but the curious thing is they must have left in a great hurry."

"How do you know that?"

"Because they left so many beautiful pots and baskets behind. Whatever the reason, they disappeared and no one knows where they went."

Julia looked down at the barren land below, feeling a little pensive. Then she nodded and said, "Yes. Disappeared. Just like the trees and shrubs along the riverbanks. Gone forever!"

"What's your guess where they went?"

"Hmmm." She looked at the river below. "Oh, probably floated down the Santa Clara River heading toward Arizona and Nevada."

"Well, they could have followed the river, but some people

think they ended up in New Mexico."

"New Mexico? Nonsense! They were washed down the river."

With a confused look on his face, John wrinkled his brow and asked, "Julia, what on earth are you talking about?"

"The trees and shrubs, of course. They all disappeared like the Anasazi Indians. Did you know that a man found his car thirty miles downstream from his home? It had crossed the border into Nevada." She turned around and faced John and saw the confused look in his eyes and asked, "What did you think I was referring to?"

John chuckled at the sudden change of subject. She had a tendency to do this to him, and he found himself befuddled many times. He often wondered if women unconsciously enjoyed keeping their men confused, just to see the bewildered look on their faces.

With a grin, he said, "Well, I thought we were talking about the Anasazi Indians, but you changed in midstream without any warning. You've got a knack of doing that to me ever since we met. The funny thing is when I actually think I've got you figured out, I realize I'm wrong. Being married to you is like a merry-go-round. I can't seem to keep up with you and get dizzy trying."

Julia smiled. "But I thought a merry-go-round is supposed to be fun."

"That's true, but trying to chase the merry-go-round is more of a challenge."

She laughed. "Just face it, John. Your first mistake is thinking you could figure a woman out. That's impossible. We think differently. We reason differently." Julia shrugged. "You're a waffle, John."

He lifted his brow with curiosity. "What did you say?"

"Waffle. That's what you are, and you can do nothing about it."

John chuckled. "A waffle?"

"Yes. That's why you can't figure us out. You see, women think like a spaghetti string, a long trail of thoughts that are interconnected, leading from one subject to another. For example, the weather makes a woman think about her clothes and what style and color would be best for the weather, etc. Or the disappeared Anasazi made me think of the trees and car that disappeared down the river." She waved her hand toward the valley with a smile.

Knowing that she had more to say, he encouraged her.

"All right, I follow. And men are waffles…"

Julia nodded. "Men, on the other hand, think in waffle pockets. Each subject has its own pocket. Women have to bring men from pocket to pocket so they can understand what we're talking about." She gave a smile of satisfaction. "Just face it, Sweetheart. Our thought process is totally different than men."

"That's for sure, in every aspect. One day you're chipper and the next you're blue. When men have a disagreement, it's done and over with and we forget about it. But women? They have to talk about it. Not only that, you expect us to read your minds. If I hurt your feelings, you won't say so, and I have to figure out what's wrong."

Julia folded her arms, suppressing a smile. "Hmmm, so you think you know us pretty well, huh?"

"Not really. Trying to understand women is difficult for men. You're very complex."

"John, we're not that complicated."

"I beg to differ…"

When her cell phone rang, John chuckled and strolled over to the roped-off archaeological site. He stuck his hands in his pockets as he studied it. Something was different from the last time he had been there. Fresh diggings were apparent, but the archaeologists had gone back to Provo four months ago. John had an uneasy feeling about it as his eyes slowly searched the site. He rubbed his chin pensively. Had they returned and resumed their research? If so, he would have to get in touch with Paul and find out.

Paul was his archaeologist friend who taught at Dixie State College. He taught history and archaeology and usually worked with the archaeologists from Provo. Both of them helped dig last summer. It was such an educational experience, and John had learned so much. He would have to get in touch with Paul this evening and see if he could help out again.

When Julia hung up the phone, she was ecstatic. She walked over to John and said with a grin, "I think I've got myself a story."

"What's the verdict?"

"They were poisoned. Matthew said it was cyanide."

"Cyanide?" John was stunned. "What on earth is this all about, Julia? Why would anyone poison fish?"

"He said that it's common to use cyanide if they want to do research on a variety of fish, but it's normally controlled. There's no indication this was controlled."

Julia's eyes had the look of determination, and he knew nothing would deter his wife from pushing ahead and finding an answer.

"John, I'm going to Gunlock."

"But the bridges aren't open yet."

"I know. The paper owns a helicopter. I want to see if anyone might know of some signs of poisoning in the area."

"Do you think your boss will approve?"

"Why wouldn't he?" she asked as she tucked her cell phone in the case. "Besides, I'll convince him. I know how to handle Bill. He's quite reasonable with a little persuasion." She grabbed her bag, slipped her hand in John's, and pulled him along. "Come on, Dear. I've got to turn in these pictures and give my little persuasion speech before he leaves work."

As they walked toward the truck, John asked, "Is everything all right at work?"

"Why?"

"I've noticed that you seem a bit stressed lately." When she didn't answer right away, he said, "I know something's bothering you. Do you want to talk about it?"

"Not really."

"Perhaps I can help."

Julia nodded. "Ted's been needling me lately."

"Ted?"

"Yeah. He's so annoying and self-centered. He always makes me feel inferior. That's why I want this story so badly. I want to prove my worth."

John instantly stopped in his tracks and swore softly. He took her by the shoulders and looked into her eyes as he said firmly, "Julia Evans, don't ever question your worth. Don't feel that you have to prove yourself to anyone. You're more valuable than you realize. And don't you ever forget it."

When John saw the stunned look in her eyes, he smiled, took her into his arms, and kissed her firmly on the lips. Then he looked into her eyes and said, "Ted's a jerk."

Julia beamed. "Don't worry. I won't let him get to me again."

He softened with her sweet smile and touched her cheek tenderly. Then remembering what a jerk Ted was, he became sober once again.

"You see to it," he said with authority. "And I mean it. You don't have to prove anything to Ted. Do you understand?"

Julia stepped backwards and saluted. "Yes, Sir!"

Then she took his hand and pulled him toward the truck.

Linda Weaver Clarke

Chapter 3

Paul was a serious sort of fellow. He was lean with blond hair and large blue eyes. His glasses were set on his long and slender nose, giving him the look of a professor. He was thirty-nine and still unmarried. As an archaeologist, he had not found a girl who could stand digging beside him all day long. Until then, he would remain single. He was a fanatic when it came to the preservation of historical sites. He was always involved in restoring the past.

Paul closed the door and escorted John into the living room. "Have a seat, John. It's so nice to see you again. What's up? When you called and asked to see me, I wondered if something was wrong."

"Well, I had to drop Julia off at her office and thought I'd stop by." Then with an accusing tone, he asked, "How long have the archaeologists been here, and why didn't you call me?"

"What are you talking about, John?"

"I was at the site today with Julia. She had to take a few pictures, so I just meandered around and saw that some recent digging has been done."

Paul's eyes widened. "Are you sure?"

"Yup, I'm sure. I looked at it real good, and it's fresh. And it looks like they've been at it for quite some time. I get the feeling you didn't know about it."

Paul's eyes became serious and his jaw tensed. "John, they haven't been down here. I know that for a fact. They're not due for another couple months. I keep in contact with them and they would have called me. I let a couple of them stay here, free of rent, while digging. Something's definitely up."

Feeling confused by Paul's tenseness, John asked, "What do you mean, Paul?"

"These are not archaeology diggers. They have a different name. You could call them pirates. Thugs. Looters. Louts."

"Louts?" asked John as he tried to comprehend the depth of this new information.

Paul gave a curt nod. His face was flushed as he gripped the sides of his armchair. He was furious and looked as if he were about to explode. This was a sensitive subject to him, and John could see he was upset.

John looked at Paul questioningly and said, "Now tell me what's going on. I'm not that familiar with these louts."

Paul spoke with more force than he intended, but he was growing more upset by the second. "In 1906, the U.S. Congress passed the Antiquities Act because the collecting of artifacts was getting out of control. It protects archaeological sites, allows research, and imposes fines and sometimes imprisonment for the vandalism of historic sites."

John's face sobered at his words.

"In other words, John, it's illegal to collect artifacts, whether on government land or private."

"Private?"

"That's right. It's been illegal since 1906, and thefts at archaeological sites are growing every year. Unfortunately, stealing isn't only among thieves."

"What do you mean?"

Paul shook his head in disgust. "Let's say a family is out hiking and finds an arrowhead. They want a souvenir for their vacation, so they pick it up and take it home with them. Is that looting?"

"Well, if it's not on an archaeological site, I wouldn't think so."

"No, you're wrong. As innocent as it may seem to the family, collecting arrowheads is illegal. If tourists come upon a bunch of Anasazi pottery shards and collect one piece, that's looting. They should give it to a nearby historic museum."

"What if it's found on private land?"

"Now that's a good question. There's no law to prevent digging on private property. In fact, archaeological thievery has gone corporate. They even pay rent on private property in order to dig without being caught. Sometimes entire pueblos have been removed. An ancient funeral pit can be sold for as high as sixty thousand dollars on the black market."

John's eyes widened at the value placed on the ancient past, something the public would never see because of greed.

"John, I'll tell you one thing. These men are armed and dangerous. That's what money does to them. They're making a lot of money, and they're ready to fight dirty for it. Money can make a person become relentless. If men like that are working at our site here, we're in for a fight. They won't give up easily. But I'll tell you one thing, they won't get away with it. The law is on our side."

John leaned forward, resting his arms on his knees and

looking intently into Paul's eyes. He cleared his throat nervously and said, "I recently read this article in the Las Vegas Newspaper. Some men were loading artifacts in the trunk of their car. A ranger saw what they were doing and questioned them, not realizing he had accidentally stumbled upon the largest operation around, sort of like a corporate company. The article said they recovered more than eleven thousand one hundred relics."

Paul slapped his hand on the end table so hard that it rocked back and forth. "That infuriates me!" he growled. "Theft of this kind is all over. At the Gettysburg National Military Park a few years ago, a man was searched and they found a metal detector hidden in his pants. He was scouring the park with it protruding from his pant leg. He was looking for Civil War relics."

"Civil war?" asked John in astonishment.

"Yeah. But Utah's vandalism is the worst in the country."

"The worst? How can that be?" John asked with surprise.

Paul immediately stood, walked over to his cabinet, and opened the glass door that held some of his samples that he used during archaeological lectures. He picked out a potshard and handed it to John.

Paul pointed to it as he said, "I visited an Anasazi site a few years ago and saw thousands of pottery shards similar to this one lying on the ground. A couple years later, I went back for a visit. I was shocked. Every piece was gone. One by one, tourists had collected them. All evidence that the Anasazi culture ever existed in that area was gone."

John gave a low whistle as he stood and handed the shard back to Paul.

"Did you know that people are actually selling these shards

and arrowheads on websites?" asked Paul.

John shook his head. "Hmmm, it sounds like the Anasazi culture is being sold to the highest bidder."

"That's right."

"What do you think we should do?"

With determination, Paul looked into John's eyes. "First off, let's take a look at the site. Catching thieves like this is usually by luck. Then we'll report it to the archaeologists in Provo, and they can have an investigator search out what's going on. Are you free tomorrow?"

"I'm on a tight schedule. I've got a client waiting for a bowie knife, but tomorrow's Saturday and I need a day off. I promised Julia that I would go with her to check out the Gunlock area in the morning. Shall we meet in the afternoon?"

"That sounds good to me. I'll pick you up at six."

John walked toward the door. As he opened it, Paul said, "Bring the Ruger."

John's eyes widened in surprise. "Why? Do you think we'll have trouble?"

Paul smiled teasingly. "No. We can do some target shooting afterwards."

John chuckled. "All right then, sounds good to me."

* * *

"So, what did your boss say, Mom?" asked April as she stabbed her fork into a piece of tender roast beef and then stuffed it in her mouth.

"Bill's going to think about it. He's worried it'll be a wild goose chase."

"What do you mean?"

"He thinks that it's an accidental spilling and nothing will come of it. He'll call me in the morning. During the meantime, I did a little research. I went to every store in town that sells cyanide. I asked if anyone had bought some lately, within the last couple months. Everyone said they hadn't sold a drop. In the winter, no one worries about pesky animals such as gophers and rats. I was really getting discouraged until I finally talked to a clerk that said he hadn't necessarily sold any, but a month ago he'd answered some unusual questions about cyanide from a customer that he'd never forget. He said the man was kind of rough looking, unshaven with yellow teeth and was chewing tobacco. He said the man spat into one of his decorative vases. That made him mad, so mad in fact, that he kicked him out of the store."

John chuckled.

"What?"

"If he was supposed to remain anonymous, he sure did a stupid thing." John snickered. "He spat into a decorative vase."

Julia smiled. "Yeah. I see your point."

"So what did he ask?"

"Very strange questions, such as how much cyanide will kill pesky animals like cats."

"But Julia," John interrupted. "The man didn't even mention fish."

"I know, but it's a start." Julia poured water in her glass and then furrowed her brow. "I bumped into Ted on the way out of Bill's office."

She took a sip of water, looking into John's eyes, waiting

for a response.

"Great! The archenemy! What did he have to say this time?"

Ted was an aspiring editor. He was self-centered, full of confidence, and always made Julia feel like she was nothing compared to his talents. He was a bachelor, quite good looking with gray eyes and short blond hair. He was in his late thirties and let everyone know that he had had many years of experience. He usually got the most exciting assignments and would boast about it, especially to Julia. The most annoying thing was that he would treat her like some amateur and figured she would never get an exciting assignment as long as he was around.

Julia tried to keep her voice even, without emotion, but it was impossible. "Ted asked me what was up. I said nothing. Then he grinned and said in his know-it-all attitude, 'Bill assigned you to the Arts Festival again this year, didn't he?' His arrogant attitude infuriated me."

April's eyes narrowed with disgust. "Mom, he makes me so mad when he acts that way, as if you didn't deserve anything better. I'd like to give him a piece of my mind."

April was the protective one in the family. She seemed to worry about her parents more than the usual child. She was twenty years old, with shoulder-length honey-blond hair, sky blue eyes, and a silky smooth complexion. She was the organized one in the family, reminding everyone of their duties. Known as a prolific reader, she had gone through different moods throughout the years, from fantasy to Jane Austen to teenage romance novels. Right now she was reading *Jane Eyre* and couldn't put it down. April was also a potter and made exquisite bowls, mugs, and vases. She also taught the art of pottery at a craft shop. She was still living at home until she could earn enough to live on her own.

Her two sisters were twins, Sharlene and Faith, and they could come up with the most mischievous ideas. They always said that two heads together were better than one. They were eighteen and students at Dixie State College. Both had dark brown hair, chocolate brown eyes, and an olive-toned complexion, just like their father.

The twins were completely opposite from one another. Sharlene was quiet and soft spoken, loved college, and studied hard. Faith, on the other hand, was the talkative, excitable, and active one. She could not sit still for the life of her, and studying was the last thing on her mind.

April stared at her sisters with indignation, "I don't understand why he thinks he's better than mom."

"Yeah!" Sharlene spoke up. "As if mom didn't have the ability to do something more challenging."

Faith asked curiously, "Mom, does he always act like he's better than you?"

"He sure does," Sharlene interjected. "And I know why. It's because she's a woman. That's why."

"No, that's not it," Faith said with a grin. "He's just afraid she might be better than him. Cowards always try to put down their competition."

"Want to know what I think?" asked Sharlene. "I think he's jealous because Mom got a book published and he didn't."

April slammed her glass down with anger, swishing her water over the edges and startling everyone. "No! It started way before the book was published. He's always treated her like he's superior, like the suave and cool man he wants to be… but isn't!"

Matthew peeked his face through the door, exposing a light smattering of freckles on his upper cheeks and across his nose. "What's up? I could hear April yelling all the way down the street." His blue eyes twinkled with mischief as he added, "I heard you mention suave and cool. Were you talking about me?"

"No, Matthew. I'm afraid not," April said, trying to control a smile playing at the corners of her lips. "You're much better than Ted by a long shot. In fact, you're quite the opposite."

Matthew grinned even wider, accentuating his dimpled cheeks as he stroked his sandy red hair with the palm of his hand in a confident manner. "I knew it. Anybody can be cool. I'm simply hot."

That got a giggle from the girls and a chuckle from John.

"You needn't say more, April. I already know how you feel about me," Matthew said teasingly as he shut the door behind him.

He walked over to her and gently mussed her hair as he passed by. Then he plopped down on a chair to listen.

Matthew was a quiet young man, a twenty-four year old chemist, a genius who graduated from high school at the age of sixteen and from college at twenty. He grew up with the girls and had become great friends. He was the protective brother they never had. In fact, he spent more time at the Evans' home than his own, and they treated him like family.

There was only one secret the family didn't know about. Matthew loved April beyond words. He was head over heals in love, but she didn't suspect anything because he didn't know how to tell her. April treated him like a kindred friend, and that was all. He wished that some day she would come to her senses and realize they could be more than friends. He believed in dreams. If you hoped hard enough, perhaps it could come true.

Julia smiled. "Are you hungry, Matthew?"

"Naw. Just came to visit. Are you having dessert?"

"Apple cobbler."

"Then I'll stay," he said as he stretched his long legs and crossed them at the ankles. "Your apple cobbler is the best in town."

John turned to his wife and asked, "So, what did you say to him, Julia?"

"Ted?"

"Yeah."

"I said it wasn't true, that I wasn't assigned to the Arts Festival, and that my new assignment was something very important. He smiled and asked what could be more important than the Arts Festival. So I told him."

"Oh, no!" John groaned slightly, covering his hand over his eyes and shaking his head. "What was his reaction?"

With daggers in her eyes, she answered, "He laughed at me and said that it was probably an accidental spilling, and I would be wasting not only my time but the paper's."

John peeked at her between his fingers and dared not say more.

"Mom," April said, trying to comfort her a little. "I just hope that Bill gives permission for this assignment and that you solve a big mystery and show him up. He needs to be humbled a little."

Julia could not help but laugh at her daughter's protective attitude.

Faith laid her spoon on the table with a thoughtful look. Then she turned to her father and asked curiously, "Why isn't mom ever given assignments like Ted?"

John rubbed his chin with a solemn expression, realizing that he needed to say something. "Well…" He cleared his throat, ready to give his opinion. "My guesstimate is that Bill doesn't want to put her into danger. And I'm glad he's so protective, but he could trust her a little more, I'd think."

Julia finished her water and set the glass on the table, keeping a firm grip around the glass as if it were Ted's neck.

As she tightened her grip, she looked at John and said, "What really made me mad was when he grinned that ridiculous grin of his, as if he were 'Mr. Charming,' and said, 'Just stick to your regular assignments, my dear, like reporting the women's fundraisers.' I just stuck my chin in the air and said, 'I wouldn't worry so much, Ted. How could I ever show you up? By the way, my name is Mrs. Evans or Julia. I'd appreciate the use of it from now on.' Then I stomped out of there and didn't say another word."

"Good for you!" Matthew bellowed and began to applaud his approval. "As April mentioned, he needs to be humbled a bit. You know, brought down a few notches!"

April grinned at Matthew and patted his shoulder.

"Well, Mom," Sharlene said seriously. "I heard there's going to be a Muddy River Relief Fund-Raiser at Tuacahn Arts Center for the people who lost their homes. Everyone's donating their time and homemade stuff. I know how you feel about this flood, but if Bill assigns you to do it, can you imagine what Ted would say?"

Julia released the powerful death grip on her glass, relaxed, and smiled. This took John aback, surprised with the softness in her eyes as he wondered what she was about to say. He leaned forward and waited. Why had her behavior changed so quickly?

"What a wonderful assignment that would be!" She looked at everyone at the table and said softly, "Yes, I can imagine his attitude. And I would reply, 'I'm so grateful that Bill assigned me to such a worthy and unselfish cause to report on.' Then I would donate three dozen books to the fundraiser to help those in need."

Chapter 4

The red mountains, rocks, and soil were all part of the magnificent landscape of Washington County. This area was known as "Color Country" because of the beautiful, deep coral-colored scenery. It was a land of dreams; full of unimaginable beauty that completely overwhelmed the soul.

Julia gazed out the window of the chopper and could see the tall mountains extend for miles and miles. In the early spring, this desert land turned green. With the red mountains as a backdrop, this country was absolutely gorgeous. The colorful desert land was filled with prickly pear cactus, the wicked cholla with its bright red blossoms, and Joshua trees with razor-sharp points. Julia wasn't too fond of the summer heat, which could reach one hundred and ten degrees or higher, but the winters were grand. Her favorite time of year was autumn, when the weather was in the seventies and the leaves turned a rusty color in the nearby mountains.

The helicopter gradually came upon Gunlock Dam, exposing a magnificent waterfall in the distance. The white-foamed water was flowing rapidly over the rocks from the overfilled reservoir, causing a mist to form as it fell to the ground. From the sky, the beauty of the blue reservoir against the rugged mountains was awe-inspiring, something a painter would sit for hours and take in. Usually, water was a welcome sight in this desert region, but it had given more than was expected this year.

John turned to his wife and said, "I've heard many people say they learned what true charity was about ever since the flood. The communities are pulling together and trying to help the flood victims, giving and helping all they can."

Julia nodded. "We've never had our faith tested like this before, have we?"

John shook his head, watching her intently. "Do you have any set plan when we get to Gunlock?"

"I'm going to interview a few people. How about you? What are you going to do?"

"I think I'll help shovel out one of the three homes that was filled with mud."

"Okay. Sounds good to me."

"This afternoon, you're on your own, though. I talked to Paul last night, and he wants to go out to the archaeological site and look at it."

"What do you think you saw yesterday?"

"Oh, it could be an animal digging something up, but I'm not sure. I should have taken a better look at it. Since we now know the archaeologists weren't here, we'll take a closer look at it this afternoon."

Julia saw the small town of Gunlock in the distance as she said, "I got the go-ahead on this project."

John smiled. "I'm glad for you. I know how much you wanted to do it."

The pilot searched for a place to set down. It did not take long until he found a flat spot. John went directly toward a bunch of men and asked what he could do to help. They immediately handed him a shovel and pointed toward a home.

Julia walked down the only road that went through Gunlock. It was a small farming community, and homes were situated on both sides of the road. She knocked on the doors and asked a few questions. The people she spoke with were kind and friendly, but they had never seen any dead fish floating in the river. She began worrying that this might be a wild goose chase after all, and she might end up with nothing. What if it was an accident after all?

After a few hours of knocking at doors and interviewing people, she finally got lucky. A young woman opened the door with a flowered apron tied around her waist and a couple of children hanging on her legs with wide, curious eyes.

The young woman frowned as if remembering something and then drawled, "O-o-oh yes, I remember. It was just before the flood. My two older boys were playing by the creek. That's all it was then, just a creek, not like it is now." She shook her head in dismay. "Well, anyway, that's when they found it. But it wasn't a fish. It was our pet cat. He died mysteriously. We were puzzled and couldn't figure out what happened. One day, it was snuggled in the arms of my son while watching TV. And that afternoon he was gone. He was a healthy pet, nothing wrong with him at all."

"Yeah," said a freckle-faced boy as he peeked around the corner of the kitchen. "That's what happened."

Julia raised her brow curiously.

He walked toward the door. "In case you need to know, that wasn't the only dead animal we found. My brother and I found a couple other cats and a dead skunk a few days before that. They weren't scuffed up like they were in a fight or nothin'. They just up and died. You know what I mean?"

Julia's eyes widened with anticipation. She was learning more than she figured she would. "Can you remember when that was?"

"No, but it was just before the flood. What do you suppose happened?"

"I'm not sure. What did you do with your cat?"

"My dad put it in a gunnysack and buried it in the backyard."

"Would it be all right if I took it to a lab and found out why it died?"

"Sure. It's all right with me."

He led Julia toward the backyard and grabbed a shovel on the way. As they walked, Julia asked a few questions about school and so forth.

"School? Hey, I can't get to school with the bridges out," he drawled out just like his mother. "It's like a vacation for me ... sorta fun, but I miss my friends. Been shoveling mud, though."

"By the way, where did you find the other animals?"

When they stopped near a mound of dirt, he looked up at Julia and said, "My brother and I were playing with our friend, Billy, who lives up the road a ways. You know... the road heading up the canyon?"

"Toward General Steam?"

"Yeah. We were all playing together when we found them. We always play with Billy after school when we finish our homework, that is, until the flood swept away the bridge and then we couldn't play no more."

He waved toward the canyon and continued, "I remember one day, this yellow Hummer went lumbering up the road toward the mountains, and it blasted its horn at us to get outta the way, almost like he was leaning on it. There's no traffic up in them mountains, so we just play wherever we please. Well, because Billy thought he was really rude to honk at us like that, he up and threw a rock at that Hummer and it skidded to a stop, making rocks go flying in all directions. It was scary."

"A Hummer?" asked Julia curiously.

"Uh-huh." He began digging as he continued with his story. "Man, he was mad. He got outta that Hummer and told us off. He was a big man, all right. And he had yellow teeth, too, just like he never knew what a toothbrush was. I remember that for sure because he looked so scary with dark stubbly hair all over his face, and he was spitting black juice everywhere. He put his fist in the air and yelled at us and then called us names and swore at us. He said we had no right being in the road like that and to get home. Then he took off, throwing gravel everywhere. It was really strange, him takin' off up the road like that."

A large man with yellow teeth who spat black juice! That was sure a coincidence!

Julia looked at the young man and asked curiously, "What's so odd about a Hummer going toward the mountains?"

"Vehicles don't go up the mountains just before it gets dark unless they plan on staying overnight." He shook his head in bewilderment. "Strange. Who would want to camp out in the cold mountains this time of year? Not only that, but Billy told me that everyday, just like clockwork, he'd come outta the mountains in the daytime and go back in the evening."

The young man stopped digging and dropped the shovel to the ground. Then he stooped down and picked up the gunnysack and shook off the dirt. The repulsive stench was horrible, and the young man quickly held his fingers to his nose as he handed the sack to Julia.

"Here it is, Ma'am. Hope you can find out what happened to him."

As the putrid, nauseating odor wafted toward her nose, Julia's stomach did a few flip-flops. She felt as if she were about to gag when she instantly held her nose with her fingers and took the sack with the other hand. With a nasal sound, she thanked the young man and headed toward the chopper in a hurry.

When she arrived at the helicopter, she found no one around, so she set the sack down and went looking for the pilot and her husband.

John and the pilot were both shoveling mud from one of the homes. The mud was a few inches thick on the kitchen floors and rugs. The walls had water stains on them, but they could be washed off or repainted.

While Julia was talking to different individuals in the community, she found there was such camaraderie and love among the people that she had never seen nor felt before. A feeling of charity for one another seemed to radiate, and she was impressed beyond words. The people were sticking together, no matter what religion or culture they were. As she thought about it, that was the whole attitude of Washington County. The people cared about one another without reservation. Charity was the secret.

Julia asked if she could do something, and one of the

women handed her a plate full of sandwiches. "Take these to the men. They're probably starving. They've been at it all morning."

Julia was grateful to be able to help in some way. She had been reporting about how the people were willing to help one another. Now, this was her chance to help, even though it seemed insignificant compared to what the men were doing. After taking several trays of sandwiches to the men, she asked her husband if he was ready to leave.

John stretched his tired muscles and wiped his brow with a handkerchief. He gave a nod, handed his shovel to the man in charge, and headed toward the chopper with Julia and the pilot.

As they slowly walked, Julia reported everything she found out. "So, you see, all this happened before the flood."

John looked at her and said, "But Julia, you don't know if the cats or the skunk were poisoned. You're jumping to conclusions."

"I know." She sighed. "But I'll ask Matthew to get started right away so we can find out if it's connected to the fish. If it is, then we're getting closer. The answer has to be upstream, perhaps up in these mountains."

As they approached the helicopter, the stench of the dead cat permeated the air, and a swarm of flies were buzzing around the gunnysack. John looked over at his wife and pulled a face of disgust.

"Julia, I take it this is our new passenger?"

She gave a weak smile. "I'm afraid so." She looked over at the pilot and asked, "Is there anything we can do?"

He burst into laughter at their dilemma. After settling down, he formed a plan. "I'll tie it to the outside of the chopper and let it dangle."

John grinned. "That sounds good to me, as long as I don't have to ride with it." He shook his head as he looked at Julia. "You've brought your work home with you before, but this really takes the cake, Julia."

Chapter 5

Paul walked around the roped area of the Anasazi dwelling, looking for evidence of recent diggings. He pursed his lips, and his shoulders tensed as he looked at John. "I would say there has been some digging done here, all right. In fact, quite a bit since we were here four months ago. And it looks like professionals have done it, too. They know exactly what they're doing."

"What makes you say that?" John asked, as he looked closer at the site, trying to see what Paul was referring to.

"First off, they haven't left any tracks. Do you see any at all?" Paul grumbled.

John looked around the ropes, inside and out, and beyond.

"No, there aren't any."

"They have picked up after themselves and swept away any evidence they were here, even their tracks."

This was all new to John, and he wasn't sure what this meant. "So, if these are professional looters…"

"I'd say we're in for trouble, John. If they've found what I suspect they have, they won't give up easily. Greed can make a person mean."

John furrowed his brow and thought for a moment as he looked at the diggings and then said, "Let's keep this quiet as long as we can. I don't want Julia finding out about it."

"Oh, I agree. I want to do this quietly so we can catch them. I don't want the media to mess up everything." Then he looked at John curiously. "Did you mean Julia specifically or the media?"

"Well, because Ted's been a jerk lately, she's determined to get a good story. Now, don't get me wrong. I want her to get a good story but not this one." He shook his head adamantly. "It's too dangerous. I know her. Once she finds out about it, Julia's curiosity will not let up, and she'll put herself into danger. In fact, I'm glad she's chasing after dead fish and cats rather than looters. I think I'll keep this quiet so she doesn't get any bright ideas. I just hope this new story pleases Bill."

Paul smiled. "John, if I could find a woman as good as Julia, I would feel awfully lucky. She's a fine lady."

"Yup, she sure is." John nodded. "So, what are you going to do first?"

"I'm going to report it to the archaeologists in Provo, and they'll probably turn it over to some investigator. I'll keep watch, though, and report whatever I find." Paul pointed to the revolver in John's holster. "Well, John. Are you up to a little target shooting?"

John grinned. "When am I ever not in the mood?"

They took off, heading down the hillside to enjoy a sport that John had loved since childhood. His grandfather, John Roberts, had taken him shooting at a very young age and had taught him how to shoot. For a long time he had admired his Grandfather's rifle. It was a 45-70 and he felt that the day he could pull the hammer back with one thumb was the day he was a man. As a boy, it had taken two thumbs. He would never forget the special times he had with his grandfather as they hunted deer in the mountains and pheasant in the meadows.

John had become a very good shot and could hit his target at two hundred yards with his Winchester 30-30 rifle. He was pretty good with his 357 Magnum revolver, also. He could hit the target dead on at twenty yards. His father didn't care for guns and tried to discourage him, but John felt it was in his blood. He was too much like his grandfather.

John meandered down the hill, chatting and joking around about the reasons why Paul was still single. "Paul, what you need is a woman who doesn't mind getting a little dust on her face. I've never known an archaeologist that wasn't dusty."

Paul laughed. "You're right. Our first date should be among the ruins and if she can handle that, then she can handle anything."

As they walked, they carefully climbed over the black volcanic rock until they hit the bottom where they would do a little target shooting against the canyon wall.

As Paul turned a corner, his eyes widened in disbelief, and he instantly halted to a stop. John bumped into the back of him with a jolt and was about to ask him what was wrong when his own eyes saw the same problem.

"Paul? What the...?" He was speechless.

"The vermin found another dwelling. I can't believe it. How did they know it was here?" Paul shook his head in disbelief, his eyes fuming with rage. "This looks like a small pueblo. Look how much they've dug already. Some of these holes are big enough to place a truck inside. They've probably taken millions of dollars worth of pottery, baskets, and whatever else they could find." He looked at John with concern. "It's worse than I thought. This could be a big corporation at work. If so, we're in for trouble because they won't give up that easily, not with this much money involved."

"What now, Paul?"

"I'll call my friends in Provo and talk with them. First, we'll put a watch on this place."

As they looked around, they found nothing of value. After an hour of searching and checking out the pueblo, they headed back with information for the archaeologists.

John realized this would be a tough one to keep secret from Julia, but he had to. He knew his wife's curiosity would get the best of her, and she would get herself into heaps of trouble. Besides, when the time was right, he would make sure she was the first one to be involved when Paul gave the word. In the meantime, could he keep a straight face?

* * *

John walked into the kitchen where Julia was cutting a few potatoes for a potato salad. He looked down at the handsome knife in his hand that he had just completed. He had forged and ground a Damascus steel blade into a beautifully shaped bowie knife and then heat-treated it. Afterwards, he polished a handsome cocobolo handle and attached it to the blade. On the side of the handle was a priceless gem.

Busting all over with pride, he was going to show it to Julia, but instead, he chuckled and bellowed out, "You call that a knife? I could cut twice the potatoes with this one and in half the time."

Julia turned around, and her eyes widened with awe at the

beautiful knife he held in his hand. His chest seemed to be bulging with satisfaction as he grinned from ear to ear.

"Why, you finished it. It's absolutely stunning," Julia gushed.

"It sure is, isn't it?"

"Who is it for?"

"A mayor in Nevada. He said he wanted a bowie knife and picked out the wood he wanted for the handle." He shook his head with annoyance. "Then he asked me to put a gem on the handle. I told him that mountain men didn't have gems on their handles, but he said he wasn't a mountain man and he wanted a gem." He shrugged. "So, I put a gem on the handle."

"What's it worth?"

John smiled. "Julia, you don't want to know. Let's say that it's worth about twice of your six-month pay at the paper."

"Oh my! What will he do with it?"

"Hang it on his wall along with the swashbuckling sword I made for him last year. He's quite the collector."

Julia grinned teasingly. "So you don't think he'll be helping his wife cut potatoes with it?"

John glanced at the knife amusingly. "No. I hate to admit this to you, Julia, but he's one of those chauvinistic males. He tells his wife exactly what he wants to eat and what time to have it on the table, and if it's not ready, then he has a fit. She does what he says, and he won't lift a finger to help."

Julia turned back to her potato salad without a word. She was not about to get on her soapbox about men who never help their wives. It infuriated her that men would not help with household chores.

John interrupted her thoughts. "This knife cost him twenty

four thousand dollars. And you know what? It isn't that much when you think about the price of some knives. Did you know that the replica of the Tut Dagger cost over one hundred thousand dollars?"

Julia's jaw dropped at the price. "Why did it cost so much?"

"Buster Warenski spent five years on the project. It was made of tempered gold, which was an art that had been dead for centuries. After many failures in casting the billet…"

"What's a billet?" she asked curiously.

"It's a metal bar that's formed into a blade. After many failures, he finally figured out the formula. The dagger was made from thirty-two ounces of gold, with enameling and gold bead work fused around the handle."

"Wow, I'm impressed."

"Well, that's not all. One collector saw it on display and wanted one just like it. Buster refused, but designed the Gem of the Orient for him instead. To make a long story short, it was made of tempered gold and had about nine carats of diamonds and over forty emeralds. It was displayed in Japan for one point twenty-five million dollars."

At this announcement, Julia's knife slipped from her hand and fell to the cabinet as she stared into her husband's face with disbelief and amazement.

He laughed at her shocked expression. "Hey, art knives are valuable, and collectors will pay the price."

She looked at the knife in his hand with a twinkle in her eyes as she asked, "So, do you want to try that twenty four thousand dollar knife out? Want to help?"

John grinned. "Sure. It's the best way to show you how this beauty works. Besides, I don't have to use this bowie knife to cut faster than you. I've always been able to outdo you when it comes to cutting veggies."

Julia burst into laughter, making John grin even wider.

The phone rang, interrupting their laughter. Julia had been waiting for two weeks now to find out about the dead cat. Matthew was too busy to do much about it. So he said he would get to it today. She was expecting a call any moment, and she could not seem to concentrate on much. When Faith answered the phone and began chatting, John knew she would be talking forever.

He gently touched Julia's shoulder and said, "I'll talk to her. Don't worry." He laid his knife down on the cabinet and walked into the living room and asked politely, "Can you keep it short? Your mom's been waiting for a call from Matthew."

Faith nodded and then he walked back into the kitchen. He took his bowie knife in hand and began cutting the potatoes. It did not take long for Julia to stop what she was doing and watch him. John had a grin on his face as he cut each potato with his fancy knife. She giggled and continued cutting.

He looked at her curiously and asked, "What?"

"Oh, it's just that knife, that's all. A person would think it was made for defending oneself instead of kitchen work."

"Hey, back in the olden days, these bowie knives were made for skinning and gutting a deer." An amused look crept into his eyes as he added, "And they would even shave with it."

John put the knife to his jaw with a grin, showing how it was done, and then flinched. "Ouch! Dad-blast it! I forgot how sharp this thing is."

After seeing her stunned expression, he laughed. "I was just joking around."

Julia slugged him in the arm, trying to hide her shocked look. "I knew that!"

He chuckled again, and she slugged him even harder that time.

After dinner, the girls decided to play a board game called "Sorry." John was reading a mystery book while Julia was pacing. She could not seem to sit still. The information that Matthew had would determine whether she was allowed to continue her story.

April looked up at her mother and said, "Mom, stop pacing. You're wearing out the carpet. Matthew will call when he's ready. I'm sure he knows you're anxious to hear the verdict."

"Besides, Mom," said Sharlene. "You're making us nervous."

"Talking about Matthew..." said Faith as she moved her man. "Matt's been working out every morning at the college gym. I walked in on him one time while he was lifting weights. He's got quite the biceps, if you know what I mean. And good looking, too." She giggled. "That is, if you like freckles and red hair."

Sharlene added, "And he's intelligent, witty, and charming." She looked out of the corner of her eye at April and smiled inwardly. "He would make some lucky woman a great catch."

"That's true," said Faith. "Kris would like to go out with him. She thinks he's quite a hunk. We could arrange it." She turned to April and grinned. "What do you think?"

April narrowed her eyes and said impatiently, "I say let's

finish this blasted game. I've got a book to read."

The twins raised a curious eyebrow.

When April saw their amusement, she blurted out, "She's not his type."

"Why not?"

"She's too quiet and mild mannered. Matt's quiet, too. They would end up hardly saying a word to one another all evening."

"Then how about Ang?" asked Sharlene. "She's outgoing and vivacious."

"It wouldn't work."

"Why?"

"Because he's not a talkative person. She would get bored with him."

"How about Di?" asked Faith.

April sighed. "She's a romantic and would expect him to bring her flowers and take her to the Shakespeare festival. He's not romantic at all, I can assure you. She would be unimpressed."

The twins looked at one another, and something passed between them as they smiled and nodded.

Faith placed her hands on her hips and asked, "Will any girl be good enough for him? Or will you find fault with each one?"

"I don't know what you're talking about," April said with irritation.

"Why don't *you* go out with him?"

April shook her head. "He's not interested in me."

"How do you know?"

"Don't be ridiculous. We're only friends. If we date, it would ruin our friendship."

"Or enhance it."

"And if we break up? Then what? We'd feel uncomfortable around each other." April shook her head adamantly. "I don't want to lose our friendship."

Faith sighed. "You're impossible." She dropped the dice on the table, moved her man, and exclaimed, "Sorry!"

"What?"

"I bumped your man off. I now get another turn." She shook the dice, moved her man to home base, and then proclaimed with delight, "Sorry! I won."

Before the girls could say another word, the phone rang and Julia rushed to answer it. It was what she had been waiting for all evening. With a sigh of relief and a smile, she hung up the phone.

"The cat was poisoned with cyanide."

The room was silent.

Finally, John asked, "Now what?"

"I'm going to write an article about it and see if anyone knows something, mentioning both the cat and the three-dozen fish that came from the Gunlock area. Afterwards, if I don't get any feedback, I'll give up the search to an accidental spilling simply because there'll be nothing more I can do. If people respond to my article and tell me of more poisonings, then I'll do more research and perhaps write another article about it, asking for more information. I think I'll give it two weeks for someone to come forth with information."

John looked skeptically at Julia, having a feeling it might end up at a dead end. *What if no one responds to her article?* He sadly shook his head. *She'll have to give up all together.*

Chapter 6

"I saw Julia's recent article in the newspaper, Bill. I just don't understand why you gave her permission to do research on such flimsy evidence." Ted leaned back in his chair with his hands clasped behind his head. "It's just a bunch of bologna, I tell you. You're just wasting your money. I bet it cost a pretty penny to let her use that chopper. Besides that, she doesn't have the experience. Look at me. I've been writing now for almost twenty years. She's only been writing for six."

"That doesn't mean she isn't talented," Bill defended. "Look at the novel she wrote. Besides, she chose to be a mother first. It wasn't until the twins were twelve when she finally decided to get a part-time job here."

"Yeah, and then you let her leave at 2:30," replied Ted, shaking his head in disbelief.

"That's because her girls got out of school at 2:45. She wanted to be there when they got home. I understand how she feels. I've got kids of my own. But since her kids graduated from high school, she's been working full time."

Ted scowled. "She's got you twisted around her little finger, doesn't she?"

Bill grinned, leaned over his desk, and said softly, "I had to give her this assignment, Ted. How do you say no to such begging eyes?"

"You're a pushover, especially when it comes to Julia."

Bill frowned and sat up straight. "She doesn't think so. She says I give you all the good assignments and won't let her do any of the exciting ones." Bill shook his head in dismay. "That's what she used on me when she asked for the cyanide incident."

"Exactly what I said! You're a pushover! She's just another pretty face. Just face it, Bill, she's wasting the paper's time and money. You know how it'll turn out, don't you? I can just see the headlines: 'Accidental Cyanide Poisoning.' Quote, Farmer Jones was desperate to get rid of gophers that were eating the roots of his fruit trees. His dog bumped the bottle, and it went tumbling into the creek. Unquote."

Ted burst into a fit of laughter, but Bill did not laugh or move a muscle as he stared at the doorway where Julia stood with her arms folded. Her body was stiff, her eyes looked like daggers, and her lips were pursed together.

Ted instantly tensed and cleared his throat. He stared at Bill as he softly asked, "She's standing behind me, isn't she?"

Bill nodded.

"Did she hear what I said?"

"I believe so. If looks could kill, you're dead already."

Ted cringed as he slowly turned in his seat. He gave a crooked smile and swallowed deeply. "I … I was just having fun. Didn't mean any harm."

"So, I'm just another pretty face? I don't have the talent that you have? I'm just wasting my time and the paper's?"

The impatience and anger in Julia's eyes was obvious, not to mention the tension in her voice. The atmosphere was

Anasazi Intrigue

heavy, and her boss wished he could just slip out unnoticed. Bill was the manager of the local newspaper, a gentle and jovial fellow. He had plenty of money and decided that building a newspaper was a good move. He had a round face, blue eyes, and gray hair that encircled his balding head. He liked Julia a lot and was a pushover at times when she would ask for a favor. Every time Julia walked in the office, he would try to stand or sit taller and suck in his belly.

Bill looked at Ted with soberness and said, "Ted, will you excuse us, please?"

Ted was grateful for the reprieve, so he quickly stood and bolted out the door without another word, shutting the door behind him.

Julia took a seat, adjusted her beige mid-length skirt, and then crossed her legs. Her lavender knit top complimented the soft curves of her figure, but her face seemed hard and unrelenting. She was not in the mood to talk.

Bill nervously cleared his throat and said softly, "Julia, you know Ted. He thinks that he's God's gift to women … and to this newspaper, as well. Don't think another minute about what he said. If I didn't think it was something worthwhile, then I wouldn't have agreed to it."

Julia's face softened. "You don't think I'm just another pretty face, then?"

Bill grinned. "Well, that's beside the point. It has nothing to do with it. You're capable and I have trust in you. You're a good reporter, Julia. That's why I hired you." He thought it was about time to change subjects. "Are you ready for the Muddy River Fund-Raiser? I heard you volunteered to sit at one of the booths."

Julia smiled. "Yes. In fact, I'm looking forward to it. I'm donating some of my books for the cause."

"Good for you. They want to raise fifty thousand dollars to give to the flood victims. I suspected you would do something about it. You're the charitable sort, unlike Ted."

"Ted?"

"Yup. When he found out that we were going to have a booth full of homemade goodies donated by all the employees, he said that he would like to go help out in the booth because his fans might like to meet him in person."

Julia nodded, trying to suppress her laughter.

Bill chuckled. "You know, he does get quite a few fan letters about his editorials."

"Yeah, and they're all single women, too."

Bill smiled with humor lacing his eyes. "Don't know about that."

Julia enjoyed talking to Bill. He acted like a father to her and would compliment her whenever she did a good job. He never treated her like an amateur, and that made her feel good about herself.

Julia stood and smiled. "Thanks for the talk, Bill."

The phone rang, and he picked it up and told the person on the other end to hold for a moment. "Julia? It's for you. Do you want to take it in here?"

"Sure," she said as she took the phone from his hand. "This is Julia Evans. Can I help you?"

A weak, scratchy voice of an old man was on the other end of the receiver. "Mrs. Evans, I read your article in the paper, and I have information that might help you. I'm Frank Jones and I live up on the road headin' toward General Steam, north of Gunlock. You indicated in your article that the poisoning was possibly coming from the river upstream near my place, and that got my attention. You see, I have a bunch of cats and they disappeared for a week or so and I didn't know what had happened to 'em. One day, two of 'em came home looking real sick, so I took 'em to a vet. They were not only pets but also real good mousers and good company for me since I live alone. They died shortly thereafter, and the vet said they had cyanide in their system."

"Cyanide?"

"That's right." The man growled, "Personally, I think it's those seedy-lookin' characters that head toward the mountains every afternoon. In fact, they stopped and yelled at my grandson sometime ago, and that made me real mad. The driver said words he shouldn't to a young boy."

"Can you describe him?"

"Sure can. I see him drive past every day, and he looks tough, a real hateful kind of feller. He's a hefty man, dark hair, and unshaven. My grandson said he's got yeller teeth, and he spat black juice outta his mouth."

She bit her lip, a habit she had gotten into whenever she felt nervous or anxious.

"Was he driving a yellow Hummer?"

"Yes, Ma'am. He was."

"Why do you think the poisoning has anything to do with these men?"

"Don't know. Just a feelin'. It's the fact that ever since the road was passable, before and after all that rain, they've been heading toward the mountains every afternoon, and then they head out in the morning. That's not normal to stay up in them mountains like that for a couple months, especially in cool mountain weather. Although, this year has been especially warm, that's for sure. It's been real pleasant lately. In fact, there's been a lot more traffic since it's warmed up. This nice lookin' Mercedes has been heading up there quite often. Well, anyway, I think they're up to no good."

"What makes you say that?" Julia asked curiously.

"It's their demeanor and attitude. By the way, I don't want any trouble from them fellers, so don't let on that I said anything. In fact, I shouldn't have said this much. They threatened my grandson for playing out on the road, so they'll threaten me if they find out what I said."

"Don't worry about a thing. This is confidential."

"I even called the police to tell them that I think something suspicious is going on up in them mountains. And do you know what? They didn't even give me the time of day. They insinuated that I was imagining things because I'm an old man, but I tell ya, there's something going on up there and it's not good. With characters like them fellers, I believe they would poison animals just for fun."

"Thanks for the information, Mr. Jones. If I have anymore questions, I'll give you a call."

After getting his number, she hung up the phone and grinned at Bill. "You know, it's been two weeks since I wrote that article and I didn't hear a thing from anyone, so I was ready to give up. I was starting to feel a little foolish. But now I have something. I'm not sure why, but I have a feeling this old man is on to something." She hesitated for a moment and then said, "Bill, next week I'm heading for the mountains after the Muddy River Relief. I won't be here Monday, in case you need to know."

"Are you sure about this, Julia? Could you be in any danger?"

"No, I'll be just fine, Bill." Julia gave a confident smile. "And I'll have the article about the fund-raiser on your desk by Monday morning before I leave."

"The fund-raiser is this Saturday. Will you have enough time to put it together before you leave?"

"Don't worry. It'll be ready." She gave a wave. "Well, I'll be seeing you, and thanks again for your support."

It was five in the afternoon, and Julia was headed home after a long and tiring day. She swung the door open and breathed in the fresh desert air with a smile on her lips. She was excited about the news the old man had given her.

As she stood at the door, she noticed a burly unshaven man with a contemptuous expression on his face. He was leaning against a car with folded arms and a beer can in his hand. He was a cold and hard-faced fellow with dark hair. His penetrating glare unnerved Julia and sent a chill up her spine. Then he smiled, showing his tobacco-stained teeth. He took a swig of beer and then tightened his grip on the can, squashing it with ease and tossing it through the window of a dilapidated car. His face sobered and his jaw became ridged as he glared at her. Then he popped some tobacco into his mouth and began chewing. He smiled with satisfaction when he saw the frightened expression on her face.

If this man was trying to frighten Julia, then he was doing a good job. Not only that, he had the same description that the clerk and the old man had given for the exception of one thing. Where was his yellow Hummer? Now he was standing here as if he was trying to intimidate her. When he spat some black juice out of the corner of his mouth, she winced. Yuck!

Julia was not about to be intimidated, and she quickly

averted her eyes, feeling uncomfortable. A sense of foreboding came over her, and she shivered as she quickly strode toward her car. Had he read her article in the paper? Was that why he was here?

Even though she did not look in the stranger's direction again, she knew his eyes were following her and anxiety filled her breast. Was this assignment making her feel a little paranoid, or was it her imagination that she was being watched?

Chapter 7

"They've done it again!" Paul yelled out of anger and frustration. "The miscreants haven't approached the pueblo all week long and finally they hit last night."

John and Paul were standing near the Anasazi site, scanning every inch of it. Paul was shaking his head in disgust. He walked around the site, eyeing it with fury and breathing hard.

He looked at John and said, "The investigator has been watching this whole area everyday for the past week. He never thought they would dig at night. He's been hiding behind these boulders." He waved his hand in the direction of the black lava rocks. "Nothing has happened all week, so the looters must have caught on."

"What does this investigator do all day?"

"Reads. He's got a book that's really exciting, full of intrigue. It's called *Anasazi Artifacts: Are They Lost Forever?*"

John chuckled. "Yeah, you archaeology nuts would think that was intriguing, wouldn't you?"

"Hey, it's an interesting read," Paul said, defending himself. "There's this one book I really want to read. It's called, *Origin of the American Indians* by Alvin Colton. You should read it. You'll get an education about this country and its people."

"I will?" asked John as he tried to control a grin playing at the corners of his lips.

Paul smiled at his friend's reaction. "At least give it a try. Right now I'm reading *The Mayas: A Lost Civilization*."

When John saw the stress in Paul's face, he sighed. He noticed that his smile just didn't seem to reach his eyes.

"You know, Paul," said John with concern. "You really need a vacation. You've been quite uptight, lately."

"I know." He pushed his fingers through his hair. "I've been thinking the same thing, myself."

Paul instantly became quiet and a far-away look appeared in his eyes.

When John noticed the distant look on his friend's face, he asked, "What are you thinking, Paul?"

He smiled. "You know what? If I had the chance for a dream vacation, I would go to southern Mexico and see the ruins, such as Chichen Itza and Coba and Uxmal. I'd meet the Mayas and see how they live. I'd…"

"You mean, rather than go to Europe and see the ancient ruins there?"

"You bet. I'd volunteer to be a guide or even work on some of the archaeological sites for a few months. Did you know they're still uncovering giant ruins and there seems to be no end to them… miles and miles of undiscovered ancient cities."

"How about Egypt? If you had a chance, which would you choose?"

"Now don't make this harder for me, John. You can't make me choose between two great archaeology sites."

John chuckled.

"Besides, my first love is here in America. I'm quite intrigued by the things I'm learning. How about you? Where would you go for a dream vacation?"

"Hmmm." John thought for a moment and then said, "I really haven't thought of it before." He looked at the site before him and asked, "So, how did they know we had someone watching the place?"

"Simple. If they're as smart as I think, they most likely had someone watching this area."

"So what's next?"

As they walked, Paul said, "We just wait. There's nothing left to do 'cause we have to catch them in the act of loading the artifacts into their truck. We need proof. I'll report it to the investigator." He kicked a rock out of his way as they approached the jeep. "By the way, want to go to Grand Gulch with me tomorrow morning? I can show you some interesting sights. There are a few Anasazi ruins that are quite impressive."

"For how long?"

"Oh, just an over-nighter."

John nodded. "I'd be glad to. Next Monday I'm going to the mountains with Julia after the Muddy River Relief."

"Why are you going this time of year? It's still chilly in the evenings."

"It's for Julia's research. I'm not sure what she'll find since it's such a large area, but I'm trying to be supportive to appease her curiosity. Personally, I don't expect her to find much of anything. I think it's a wild goose chase, if you ask me."

"Have you told her about the artifacts yet?"

John rested his arms on the top of the jeep. "Of course not! She'd go after this like a hungry piranha. I don't want her getting hurt."

"Good, because the investigator wants it to be hush-hush right now so he can do his job more efficiently. When he gives approval for the media to have the story, I'll make sure Julia is the first one to get an interview." Paul opened the door to his jeep and then looked at John and said, "So, when did you say you were going to the mountains?"

"Monday." John opened his door and slid in the passenger side. "It'll be fun. Just the two of us! Don't get me wrong, I love having the kids live at home, but you don't get much privacy in the evenings. In fact, we haven't had any time to ourselves for a long time because of my schedule. I'm really looking forward to it."

Paul shut the door and turned the key. "Just take your cell phone with you in case I need to get in touch with you."

John burst into laughter. "Are you kidding me? I'm trying to get Julia to leave hers home so she won't be tempted to call into work. We need some special time together ... you know, a little romantic time."

Paul stared at John and then smiled one of his crooked smiles and shook his head. "You amaze me. After twenty-some-odd years, you still act as if you're in love."

"I am!" exclaimed John.

Paul laughed, pushed on the gas and the Jeep sped down the dusty road toward the highway.

* * *

April was fiddling with a mysterious envelope marked with the word "urgent." What was inside, she was not sure, but she suspected what it might be. She had a satisfied look on her face as she grinned at her sisters.

"What's that?" asked Sharlene.

"I'm not sure, but I suspect it's good news," April said as she laid it on the table. "I've got a sneaky suspicion what it is and Mr. High and Mighty will have to eat his words."

Matthew had just entered the malt shop when he heard the tone in her voice. "Sorry ladies, I didn't mean to be late. Have you been waiting long?"

April turned and smiled teasingly. "We have. I can't believe you've kept us waiting. We were just about to give up and order without you. I don't understand why you can't be on time for once…"

Matthew held up his hand to defend himself and then hesitated when he saw the twins grinning and shaking their heads. He instantly flipped April on the shoulder and pulled her hair.

"Don't you give me any guff, Missy. You're always late and I usually have to wait for you."

April grinned. It was so much fun teasing Matthew. He was just like family to her, like the older brother she never had. They grew up together. When she struggled with a few subjects in school, he helped her with homework. Now they were grown, and their friendship was still solid.

After everyone ordered their meal, April began tucking the envelope into her purse.

"What's that?" Matthew asked, pointing to the envelope. "And why the attitude when I arrived? Who's going to eat his words?"

April grinned. "Ted's going to. I think this envelope has news about Mom's article."

"How did you get it?"

"Mom told me to pick it up from the office. The secretary called and told her that a messenger had dropped it off and said it was important that she get it immediately. I was going to invite her to have lunch with us, but she's getting ready for the fund-raiser tomorrow."

"So, you think it's a clue to all this mystery that your mom's investigating?"

"Of course."

Matthew nodded, excited to know what was inside that envelope. "Do you think she'll mind if we open it?"

"She might. Mom should be the first to read the good news."

"She's going to the mountains with dad," said Sharlene. "She seems to think the answer might be upstream."

"I know," said Matthew. "Your mom asked me to meet her in the mountains. She wants me to take some samples of the water and soil. I won't be staying long, though. It should only take a couple hours."

"How do you know where she'll be?" asked Faith.

"Oh, the usual. You know, a bunch of rocks piled up high alongside the road, giving me the message to turn at that spot. It shouldn't be hard."

All talk died down as the waitress brought their food.

April checked her burger and groaned. "Matt, could you please hand me the catsup and mayonnaise? They never put enough on for my taste."

As he passed the catsup, his fingers brushed against hers. He swallowed, trying to ignore the fluttering of his heart. Matthew knew his feelings for April had been changing from friendship to something deeper during the past year. When he realized what was happening, he hadn't said anything to her.

He knew April only thought of him as a friend and nothing more. Oh, how he wished she could see him differently!

Lately, April's touch had been having an effect on him, sending a thrill right through him that traveled straight to his heart. Every time she smiled at him, his pulse picked up speed. He noticed how the lilt of her laughter brought an everlasting joy to his soul and then he would quickly think of something else to say to make her laugh again. Most of his jokes were lame, but she seemed to enjoy them just the same.

How could he deal with these feelings, he wondered. He knew if he told April how he felt about her, it could change their relationship. And if she weren't ready, it would be quite awkward to be around her. The solution? He had to wait.

"Uhm, mayonnaise please?" April asked. "Hey, Matt, are you in a world of your own?"

He shook his head and slid the mayonnaise toward her but didn't say a word. Then he took a bite of his hamburger and watched April as she spread the mayonnaise on her bun. She was so beautiful today. Her sky blue eyes were animated when she spoke and her silky fair complexion seemed to have a healthy glow. April's wavy hair hung gently about her shoulders, and the scent of it smelled like sweet lilac blossoms. How he cherished this young woman! He loved everything about her: her sweetness, her motherliness toward her sisters, her teasing ways, and her love for creating pottery.

Matthew had never seen such beautiful creations as hers. She made vases, plates, cups, saucers, and bowls of every kind. Not only that, she created her own colors instead of buying them ready made.

Sensing his eyes upon her, April looked up and smiled.

"What's wrong?"

Matthew's mind went blank. She had taken him off guard. For the first time in his life, he failed to have a clever answer ready.

"I… You… Me… Uh… You see…"

"Yes?" April asked with an uplifted brow.

He felt his face warming up and he quickly wiped his brow with a napkin lying next to his burger. "Well, I really like your pottery."

"My pottery?" April smiled, wondering why he was thinking of pottery at a moment such as this. "Why thank you, Matt."

The twins had been watching Matthew and his reaction. They looked at one another, and something passed between them. Each knew what the other was thinking. They saw Matthew blush when April caught him staring at her. Faith grinned. Sharlene nodded.

Matthew blushed even redder.

April seemed oblivious of what was going on.

Chapter 8

Julia heard April's car pull into the driveway. She had asked her daughter to stop off at the newspaper to pick up an envelope for her. In the meantime, Julia was rounding up a bunch of books to give as a donation for the fund-raiser. She was also getting a few items together for the booth to make it look attractive and more appealing to the public.

As April walked through the house, she held the envelope in her hand. "Here it is, Mom."

Julia quickly took the envelope. Her heart was pounding with excitement. This would be her second contact. She ripped it open, unfolded the letter, and read it silently. As she read, Julia's eyebrows furrowed and her face paled. She frowned as she bolted toward the phone and dialed the newspaper office.

"Hello, Marcie. Who delivered this envelope?" She listened as her lips pursed tightly together and her shoulders tensed with stress. "No, it's not signed. Thanks, Marcie. Good-bye."

After hanging up, April asked, "What's wrong?"

"Nothing."

"Don't say it's nothing when I know it's something," April replied in a firm tone.

Julia hesitated, wondering if it were wise to tell her daughter what was in the envelope. When she saw the concerned look in April's eyes, she knew that it was useless to hide it from her. She would persist until she found out what was going on. Julia sighed. April was too much like herself…stubborn and strong willed.

"All right. You can't say anything to your father or he won't let me do this," Julia pleaded.

April's eyes widened. "What's this all about, Mom?"

"Promise?"

Julia's face was sober and her eyes intense as she waited for an answer.

April stared at her mother, wondering what was so secretive. Just the idea that her mother was keeping a secret made her more curious, so she agreed. "Okay, I promise. Now tell me."

Julia handed the note to her daughter and noticed her mouth drop as she read the message.

"Mom, you should show this to Dad. It isn't right to keep it from him. He needs to know."

"If I tell him, he won't let me continue my search. You know your dad. He's overly protective. I know he cares, but it's only between you and me. Got it?"

April frowned, not liking it one bit. "Got it," she said reluctantly. "Now you be careful, Mom. This is a real threat, you know. He says here, 'Nosey reporters can get hurt. Poisoned fish has nothing to do with you. Let it lay!' Who delivered it?"

Julia sighed. "Marcie said some kid brought it in, acting as an errand boy."

"Oh. That doesn't help much."

Anasazi Intrigue

When Julia saw April's concern, she wrapped her arm around her shoulder and said, "I'll be careful. Don't worry about me. Besides, your Dad will be there. I also asked Matthew to come for a couple hours on Tuesday to get soil and water samples so we can figure out where the poison is coming from. According to the information I got from an elderly man, these men may be polluting the water. This is my big chance for a good story. It may not be much, but it's better than doing an article on the arts festival for Easter weekend."

* * *

John and Paul stood in the dry desert land of southeastern Utah at Grand Gulch, viewing a small Anasazi pueblo. They were under a cliff where sturdy ancient rock homes were once built right into the side of the cliff. This was the first time that John had seen a site such as this, and he was overwhelmed by the feeling of reverence and respect as he listened to Paul explain the significance of a kiva.

John was staring down into a hole in the ground. At his feet were four large slabs that seemed to be cemented in place, forming a square opening with a wooden ladder protruding from the hole.

Paul was telling him the true meaning of a kiva. "You see, John, a kiva is a spiritual place, much like a church for teaching and learning. Each clan had its own kiva, and the oldest male member was the patriarch. He taught his loved ones the traditions and legends that were handed down from generation to generation."

Paul waved to the hole in the ground. "You notice the

entrance to this kiva is square, and that's because they believe evil cannot go through a square hole. Evil travels in a circular form; therefore, a square entrance will only admit a good spirit. It also represents great spiritual homes of the past, such as the pyramids in Mexico and Central America that have a square top."

Paul carefully climbed down the ladder and John followed. The large, round room was made of rock covered by thick layers of clay. Black smoke from the ancient past covered the walls and ceiling, and the room smelled musty.

"This kiva is referred to as the 'Perfect kiva' because it's the only undamaged one ever discovered," said Paul. "In ancient times, a kiva was used to teach and conduct religious practices, pray for God's blessings before the hunt, pray for rain, and bless his people with an abundant harvest. A kiva was also used for social gatherings."

In the center of the room was a small hole in the ground edged with rocks, giving it a sense of importance.

John knelt beside the hole and asked, "What is this used for?"

"It's called a Sipapu. The kiva represents the journey of life, and the Sipapu represents birth into this world. This room represents three different levels: birth, death, and the spirit world."

John was astonished at the religious beliefs the Indians had. "I never realized they were such a spiritual people."

"Oh, they had a strong belief in God. Every tribe has a name for him. Have you ever heard of Maasaw, Kukulcan, and Quetzalcoatl?"

John rose to his feet. "Wasn't Quetzalcoatl an ancient God of the Aztecs?"

Paul nodded as he stuck his hands in his pockets and said, "That's right. Kukulcan is the Mayan God, and Maasaw is the Hopi God. All three are similar in many ways. They believe he's the Creator of the World. The Indians talk about this great white bearded god that descended from the sky many, many years ago and came here to the Americas. He supposedly taught them great principles to live by and blessed their little children. Before he left, he told them that he would return one day."

"I remember hearing about that."

"Here's a bit of trivia for you. Quetzalcoatl means 'Feathered Serpent.'"

"Feathered Serpent? Why was he called that?"

Paul grinned, enjoying this so much, teaching what he loved most. "There's an old Indian legend that explains it. The quetzal is a gorgeous Central American bird with brilliant green and red plumage and has long streaming tail feathers. This beautiful bird was called the 'Lord of the Skies.' The serpent was known as the 'Lord of the Earth.' It's symbolic."

John nodded. "I've heard that the Indians use symbolism a lot."

"True. The symbol of a snake represents God's condescension to walk among us lowly men. In other words, he was lowering himself to the level of the people. The feathers represent his ability to ascend toward heaven. So, the lord of both earth and sky was thought of as the 'feathered serpent.' This was the highest title the ancient Indians could think of."

"How about you, Paul?" John asked curiously. "Do you believe that Maasaw came down from heaven?"

"I'm not sure," said Paul. "This legend has been handed

down from generation to generation. The patriarch of each clan teaches that Maasaw promised to return and when he returns, the dead will rise and be reunited with their loved ones, and peace will abide for eternity."

A warm feeling of reverence seemed to engulf John from the inside out, as he listened to Paul. He slowly climbed up the ladder with more respect for these ancient people than he ever felt before. He knew nothing of the Anasazi people before now. It was here in this kiva that the patriarch taught his family sacred teachings and principles.

As he climbed out of the kiva, John felt a sense of longing to understand these people and their beliefs. They had strong religious beliefs, and the patriarchs taught their families regularly in a spiritual atmosphere called a kiva. How much different were they than other children of God?

Chapter 9

The following morning, Julia was up bright and early, getting ready to leave for the Muddy River Fund-raiser at Tuacahn. She was supposed to be there an hour early and had volunteered to stay most of the day.

Julia had hoped to see John before she left. He had not made it back from Grand Gulch yet, but she knew he was on his way home. It was time for Julia to leave, so she slid into the car and headed toward Tuacahn.

When she arrived, Julia grabbed her box of stuff and walked up the long, slanted steps toward the outdoor area where all the activity was taking place. They had quilts, jewelry, food, and paintings by local artists for sale. A variety of musical talent would perform as background music. There was a Children's Corner with animal balloons, face painting, a beanbag throw, and storytelling by Red Mountain George. He was well known for dressing up in his Mountain Man regalia and telling tales.

Julia walked to the booth, which had already been put together for the newspaper. The desserts from the employees were placed on an attractive tablecloth, so all Julia had to do was organize the stuff she brought. All proceeds would be given to the fund-raiser committee for the people who had lost their homes.

A gray-haired lady smiled at Julia and said softly, "Everything's ready, my dear. Everyone brought the goodies they promised, and any extras are piled under the table. Good luck."

She gave a wave and off she went. Julia hadn't been there long when Ted arrived and stood beside her.

"So you're in charge of the goodies, huh?" he asked with a smirk.

Julia nodded, ignoring his attitude of superiority.

A few people walked up to them, bought goodies, and asked a few questions, such as past editorials they had written, prices for putting advertisements in the paper, and what one had to do to get an opinion published.

A young, attractive woman bought something from Ted, batting her eyes and flirting the whole time. He seemed to enjoy the attention, feeling quite important as he answered all the questions he could. He was convinced that he was God's gift to women.

That afternoon, John finally walked up to the booth to order a plate of raisin oatmeal cookies, but Julia didn't notice him as she spoke to an elderly woman. Ted took the money since Julia was busy answering questions.

"So, Ted, how's it going?"

"Pretty good. We've sold quite a bit."

John looked over at Julia as she answered the many questions given her. She was wearing a mid-length skirt with a knit top. Julia's soft auburn hair touched her shoulders and was pulled away from her face with clips. Her cheeks and lips were rosy, and there seemed to be a happy glow in her eyes. John knew that she enjoyed talking to the public, and she loved writing for the paper. She just wanted to get ahead, get a promotion, that's all. He couldn't fault her for that.

John smiled. Julia was absolutely lovely, and he had missed her during his two-day jaunt. After she answered the lady's question, he put his arm around her waist, gave her a quick kiss on the cheek, and said, "Missed you!"

She instantly turned around in surprise and smiled. "You're back. How did it go?"

"I really enjoyed myself. You doing okay?"

Julia nodded. She was not about to tell him that she received a threatening note while he was gone. She had things under control and felt safe enough. She was around people day and night. What could happen?

John looked around at the booths and said, "I'm going to look at a few items and then I have to go to work. I have a few things to catch up on before we leave Monday."

When Julia saw the glow in his eyes, she commented, "You seem happy. I guess you really needed this trip."

"It was incredible, Julia. I'll have to tell you all about it tonight. I learned so much from Paul."

John had always looked up to Paul as a great educator and always wanted to learn from him. He couldn't have had a better friend. He turned and headed toward a nearby table.

After looking around for some time, he saw a basket full of objects. He pulled one out and chuckled. Julia watched him with interest and wondered what he was grinning at. She turned to Ted and asked him to look after the booth, which he was delighted to do. That, in itself, was quite amazing. She had never known him to enjoy fund-raisers at all. He always made fun of her when she had to do an article on one.

Julia walked up to John and slid her hand through the curve of his arm. "I saw you laughing over here. What did you find?"

"Oh, something I'm going to definitely buy."

"What?"

"Dice."

He showed it to her and she corrected him, "One piece of dice is called a die. Two are called dice."

"Oh? Well, you'll die laughing when you see what's written on this one."

Julia grinned at his play on words, shaking her head at his humor.

He held his palm out and showed it to her. "It says, 'Yes, No, Definitely, Try Again, Maybe, Not Now.'" He cleared his throat dramatically and said with confidence, "I can solve any problem with this die. When the girls quarrel, I'll just toss the die. And ta-dah!" When Julia laughed, he explained. "Remember when Faith wanted to borrow Sharlene's clothes the other day, but Faith wouldn't let her? This can solve any argument."

"You think it'll be that easy with girls?" Julia shook her head in disbelief. "Dream on!"

"I didn't say it would be easy, but I think it would bring a little humor into our family."

He grinned and told the lady at the booth that he was buying the die. He handed her two dollars and then whispered to Julia, "I can even use it when we're disagreeing, don't you think? We could end many an argument with this."

Julia slugged him. "As I said ... in your dreams! When there's an argument, let me throw it and the correct answer will appear. I promise you."

Anasazi Intrigue

John chuckled and followed her to the booth, shoving the die in his pocket. "I'm going to check out the oil paintings and then I'll see you at home later tonight. Got lots to do before we leave."

Julia smiled as she watched him walk away. She loved him beyond words. Looking down at the booth, she saw an envelope with her name printed on it in bold letters. Her pulse picked up speed, and she became pale as she stared at her name. It was the same handwriting as the envelope she had received from April. She jerked her head up and started scanning the area, looking around to see who had dropped it off. People were everywhere.

She quickly ripped open the envelope and read, "Remember what happens to nosey reporters. Snooping around can get you into trouble. You've been warned once. This is twice. I'll warn you a third time for good measure."

The ache in her chest grew until she could scarcely breathe. Who was warning her to "lay off" and why? If her heart could pound any louder, it would have drawn attention. She looked around, feeling like she was being watched. When someone tapped her back, she jumped and gasped.

"Hey, what's wrong?" said Ted. "It's only me. You're a little edgy, aren't you?"

Julia smiled and ignored his comment. She sat down on a folding chair and let her eyes wander. As she scanned the area, she saw an unusually tall man dressed in white baggy pants and a jacket. He had long brown hair that was tied back in a ponytail. The sides were gray and he seemed to be in his early sixties. How could she forget him? He was the same man she saw at the Santa Clara River.

What made her stop and take notice was his demeanor.

He seemed not only self-confident, but he was smiling at her. Was he just being friendly, or was he the one who had placed the note at her table? Or was it just an accident that their eyes met at the same time?

Julia smiled and quickly averted her eyes, trying to figure out if he were friend or foe. After a minute, she looked back and he was gone. Was she just being paranoid and he was an innocent bystander? She got after herself for letting her imagination go wild and quickly stuffed the note into her purse under the table. Whoever it was probably sent another messenger like before. She told herself to relax and tried to calm her nerves, but it did not help one bit when John laid a hand on her shoulder and made her jump out of her skin.

"What's wrong, Julia?"

"She's a little jumpy today, I'd say," Ted said nonchalantly.

"Oh, it's you!" Julia exclaimed with a sigh. Her face was pale and she could not seem to cover the anxiety she felt. "I thought you were going home."

"I was, but I thought I'd say one last good-bye. Julia, you look like you saw a ghost or something."

"Oh no, I'm fine. I'm just a little tired. I've been here all day standing on a cement floor. That's all. My back is achy, not to mention my feet." She took a deep breath to help relax the tenseness around her shoulders. "The fund-raiser is almost over. I'll be heading for work in a little while. I need to write up an article. I'll be home late tonight. Don't wait up."

"Tonight?"

"Since I won't be here on Monday, I have to get it done and on Bill's desk."

"Okay." He hesitated. "Are you sure you're all right?"

"Yes, quite sure."

John nodded hesitantly and then walked away, feeling uneasy, knowing she was hiding something from him but not sure how to get it out of her. When he touched her, she had stiffened and turned pale. What was going on? As he walked down the long steps toward the parking lot, he vowed to have a long talk with her when she got home that night. Something was not right.

After another hour, Julia packed the few leftovers that remained and asked Ted to take them to a needy family while she headed for work. Even though the office was closed on Saturdays, she knew others were doing the same thing, so she would not be alone.

* * *

As Julia drove toward St. George, her mind was racing, wondering why she was receiving threatening notes. What was she investigating that posed a threat to others? Had she hit on something bigger than she realized? After a few minutes, she noticed a white Mercedes following her a little too closely. She slowed down for him to pass, but the car continued following. She peered into the mirror to see who was driving. She instantly gasped and a cold chill went down her spine.

It was Mr. Ponytail himself. Was it just a coincidence, or was he following her?

No, she was just being paranoid. She turned her attention to the road ahead and refused to look in the mirror. When she heard the Mercedes pick up speed, she glanced in the mirror just as she felt her car jolt forward. Julia's body smashed against the seatbelt around her chest, and her eyes widened with disbelief. Mr. Ponytail had rammed her bumper.

Julia felt anxiety rising within her as she felt another violent bump jolt her body forward. She quickly looked in the mirror and he was grinning. Panic began to envelop her. Was that what these sort of people did, grin so their victims would panic? Was this the third warning he mentioned in the note?

Blood rushed to her face, and her pulse throbbed like mad. Her brain worked feverishly for an answer, anything to get out of this situation. An idea popped into her mind as Mr. Ponytail aggressively bumped her car a third time. Gripping the steering wheel tightly, she quickly stepped down on the accelerator and sped toward town, hoping that she could make it before he bumped her once again.

The Mercedes was catching up, so she pressed down on the pedal harder, barely making it around the bends and curves of the road, screeching at every turn. It did not take long before she came upon the first intersection that entered town. Just as the light turned red, instead of stopping, she ran the light, hoping to get away from her assailant. The tires squealed as she turned the corner, and she breathed a sigh of relief when she saw him stop at the light.

It worked perfectly. She had made the right move, and he was not able to follow because of the traffic. Relief spread through her as she slowed down and headed for the office.

After parking in the lot near the newspaper building, Julia looked down at the steering wheel. Her hands were still gripped tightly around the wheel, and her knuckles were white from the tension. She wondered if she would have to pry her fingers loose. She took a few deep breaths to relax the tension in her shoulders and especially so she could release her iron grip from the wheel.

When she finally walked into the building, Marcie asked, "What are you doing here on a Saturday?" She looked at her pale face. "Are you all right? You look a little shaken."

"No, I'm just fine, Marcie. I'm a little tired. Don't worry. I shouldn't be long. How about you?"

"Oh, trying to catch upon some stuff. I'll be leaving soon."

Julia headed for the newsroom without another word and collapsed in her chair. Her hands and arms were still shaking, and she tried to will herself to relax. She was safe and needed to take her mind off what had just happened. She took a deep breath as she turned on her computer to begin the report.

An hour later, Marcie peeked in. "It's late. I'm going home. I'm the last one to leave, so I'm locking up. Will you be all right?"

"Sure. I've got a key."

Julia was not done. Her mind seemed to be blocked, and she was having a tough time putting her thoughts into words. She wanted to sound eloquent, but it was not working at all. Well, if she was going to take a few days off, she had to get everything done before she left. Julia knew she was tired. She had not slept well last night since her husband had gone to Grand Gulch, and standing on her feet for several hours had done her in.

Julia stood and stretched her weary body and then walked into the lunchroom. In the corner was a very inviting piece of furniture. She walked to the couch, sat down, and slipped off her shoes. It felt so good. She leaned back to relax and closed her eyes to rest for just a few minutes.

After several hours of sound sleep, she woke up and stretched every tired muscle in her body. Looking at her watch, her eyes widened as she exclaimed aloud, "Eleven o'clock!"

How had time passed so quickly? Her husband and children would be worried about her. She would have to finish early Monday morning. Julia instantly slid her feet into her shoes. Then she stood on unstable feet, slowly walked toward her desk, and turned off the computer. After grabbing her purse, she headed for the front door and locked it tight behind her.

The sky was clear and the stars were bright, giving a peaceful feeling to the atmosphere. How she wished the parking lot had lights! The only light she had was the moon and the nightlights inside the building. She should have brought her flashlight.

Julia breathed in the fresh cool air. When her stomach rumbled, she realized she hadn't had supper. Hopefully, April had saved some food for her. She was starved.

As she walked toward the parking lot, she heard the faint sound of footsteps behind her. Feeling a little paranoid, but for a good reason, she picked up speed. As she picked up speed, so did the person behind her.

Julia's heart throbbed against her chest and fear overtook her. She began to breathe deeply, trying to get her wits about her. She pictured Mr. Ponytail, and she began to feel faint. Then she pictured Mr. Yellow Teeth, and she tensed. Gripping the keys in her fist, she walked faster and so did he.

Julia could feel the stress building up inside her as she

listened to the sound of the footsteps approaching, getting closer with each step. Should she turn and face her assailant or scream and get someone's attention? As she scanned the lot in front of her, she realized there was not a soul who could help her. She was on her own.

When she heard the sound of the man's footsteps gaining on her, Julia squeezed the keys between her fingers. And then she remembered the panic button on the remote. Instantly, she pressed the button, and the car began honking out of control. The loud, obnoxious sound would attract attention easily to any passersby. She could not tell if it had worked, but she hoped the assailant would not approach a honking vehicle and would give up.

Linda Weaver Clarke

Chapter 10

Julia only had a few feet to go, so she pressed the unlock button to the car. Just as she clutched the door handle, the man grabbed her around the waist. She gasped. Without hesitation, she looked down at the assailant's soft-soled shoes and immediately stomped down, grinding her heel into his foot.

The assailant yelped in pain and released the hold he had on her. Then, with all the strength she could muster, Julia swung her elbow backwards into his diaphragm and he bent over in pain, groaning and moaning as he hugged his arms to his chest.

She spun around and swung her purse, smacking his head repeatedly with all the strength she had. The assailant yelped in pain, bending toward the ground as if helpless to defend himself.

"Ouch! Ouch! Stop! Stop! What are you doing?"

A familiar voice came from the ground where her assailant was crouched with his hands over his head. He cussed, using a few choice words, and Julia instantly recognized that voice.

"It's me! Your husband! What are you doing?"

Julia was in shock for a few seconds as John slowly rose

up and looked into her face, his expression full of pain and anguish. She felt confused and wondered what he was doing here.

By the light of the moon, John could see the fear in her eyes and then it was replaced with confusion. After a moment, he could see that she was instantly relieved to see him. But why was Julia acting as if she were in danger? Something was definitely wrong.

Rubbing the crown of his head, John asked, "What's wrong, Julia? Why did you attack me?"

She could not speak. Her body was stiff and tears began to well up in her eyes. She had no answer for the way she was acting.

When John saw how emotional she was, he immediately enfolded her in his arms and held her tight. He realized that she had been frightened senseless.

John held her close and whispered, "Julia? What's wrong? I've never seen you like this before."

Julia shook her head. She didn't want to talk about it at the moment. As he held her lovingly, Julia's thoughts strayed to her dilemma. Should she tell him the truth, and would he tell her to abandon her research? She had always been truthful to him. Julia knew she had to tell him, but she wanted to make her own decision. It had to be her choice.

When John noticed her breathing had evened out and the stiffness in her body was leaving, he tucked his finger under her chin and lifted her face toward his and asked, "What's up?"

Knowing what she had to do, she answered, "John, get in the car and we'll talk."

He opened the car door and let her in and then stepped

around to the passenger's side and slid in.

"All right, Julia. I'm ready."

"First, what are you doing here?"

"I was worried about you. You looked tired at the fundraiser, and it was getting very late. Plus, I wanted to surprise you."

"Yes, you did that." She tried to muster a smile and then added, "But please warn me before you surprise me again this late at night. Okay?"

John grinned. "Then it's not a surprise if I do." He pointed toward his vehicle and continued, "I was sitting in my truck when I saw you heading toward the car. I was going to surprise you, but I couldn't figure out why you were walking so fast. I could barely keep up with you. When I heard the car honking like mad, I figured you must have hit the wrong button again."

John remembered the last time she had pushed the panic button and couldn't make it quit. Just for fun, he made her think that she had broken the remote.

He grinned and his eyes brightened at the memory. "I figured, instead of unlocking the car, you must have pushed the wrong button. I just trotted up to help out. And to my surprise, you started beating on me." Squinting at her suspiciously, he asked, "What's going on, Julia?"

She bit her lip, trying to figure out how to approach this without making him panic. What was she saying? She was panicked! Why wouldn't he be?

Julia took a deep breath and began, "I'll tell you everything, but you have to promise that you won't tell me what to do and we'll work this out together. Understand?"

John cautiously nodded, feeling a bit confused and not

understanding what he was agreeing to. Besides that, whenever Julia bit her lip, he knew she was nervous.

Julia opened her purse, searched through the debris, and then handed him both notes. John turned on the car light and read each one. His eyes widened with anxiety as he realized what was going on. Julia had gotten herself in way deeper than either of them had suspected.

He looked up at his wife, his brows creased in a frown. "Do you have anything else to share with me?"

Julia nodded and told him about Mr. Yellow Teeth and how he had been watching her from the parking lot. All John did was nod. And then she told him how Mr. Ponytail had chased her and bumped her car several times. His jaw stiffened, but he was silent through it all, allowing her to tell him everything without interruption.

"Is that all?" John asked.

She nodded.

"Were you planning to keep this from me?"

She hesitantly nodded again.

John's lips pursed together with agitation. "Why?"

"Because you'd worry."

"Yup, you got that right," he blurted out impatiently. "But as it was, I was already worrying about you." His voice was firm and unbending. "Any more surprises before I say something?"

The stubbornness in her eyes appeared as she answered, "No, but I don't want you to tell me what to do. I want to continue the search."

John's brows knit together as he narrowed his eyes. "So, you were more worried that I'd interfere than the danger you'd be in?"

"Yes."

John thought for a moment, looking into her eyes, wondering what made this stubborn and strong-minded woman tick. What was she thinking by keeping this a secret? Why didn't she trust him? He shook his head in dismay, trying to think of appropriate words to say. She had kept this from him because she feared he would not support her. What could he say? She was right.

John shook his head in frustration and then felt his diaphragm. It was still sore and so was his throbbing foot. Her heel had dug right into it and twisted, not to mention his sore head where the metal parts of her purse hit and scratched his scalp and hands. She was one tough woman, and he had never seen this side of her during their twenty-some-odd years of marriage. But then, she never had to show it before either.

John looked into her eyes and saw the anticipation in them, waiting for his answer. He grinned as he looked at her and gently rubbed his belly and said, "Julia, you have one wicked elbow, and you think fast, too. I pity the poor man who tries to walk up behind you next time. I'll support you in this, but no more secrets. Got it?"

Julia smiled broadly. "Thanks, John."

"Promise me? No more secrets?"

"Of course."

"Okay. Now listen to me. What if we would have gone into those mountains Monday and I didn't know a thing about this? How would I be able to defend us without adequate knowledge? I'm not sure what kind of men these are, but if they would have approached us and threatened me, I wouldn't have been ready. Now I'm mentally prepared to defend us if the need arises. I won't be surprised. Do you understand what I'm saying? I wouldn't have been prepared and would have been defenseless. Do you realize that?"

"I didn't think that far ahead," she said meekly.

"Obviously!"

Julia could tell he was frustrated. He had spoken more firmly than usual, and he was worried about her.

"John, I'm sorry."

"No harm done." Then he rubbed his belly and groaned. "Correction. Let me rephrase that. We've got to be more honest with one another from now on, all right?"

Julia could see he was still tense, so she slid closer to him and asked, "You all right?"

"Yeah, sure," he muttered unconvincingly.

"Want me to make strawberry shortcake for a midnight snack? I've got some frozen strawberries."

John looked into her eyes and chuckled. "Are you trying to butter me up with food?"

"Yes, I believe so. I think you need it."

"Julia?"

"Hmmm?"

"I would never forgive myself if anything happened to you."

When Julia heard the concern in his voice and saw his brow furrow in thought, she asked, "What's wrong?"

"You can trust me," John said. "Don't ever lie to me. Please."

"I never have, John," she said defensively. "I just didn't tell you everything. That's not lying."

"When you leave pertinent information out, it's on the edge of lying."

"I don't like your definition of lying," she said firmly, feeling insulted that he would even suggest such a thing. "I would never lie to you and you know it."

"Okay. Let's just say that you withheld very important information."

When she didn't answer, John realized that he should change the subject. The last thing he wanted to do was hurt her feelings and start an argument. He had been gone for a couple of days and had really missed her.

With a grin, he said jovially, "Hey, Julia! Remember that little wooden die? Let's try it out."

"What do you mean?"

"You know, just for fun. I want to test it and see if it really works."

Julia relaxed at his cheery smile and watched him reach into his pocket and pull out the die.

After unwrapping it, he said, "I've been gone for a couple days and have really missed my wife. Will she agree to a session of good old fashioned making out?"

Julia burst into laughter. "Making out?"

Watching her laugh made him smile from ear to ear as he said, "That's right. My Grandpa use to call it *spooning*."

"My dad called it *making whoopee*," she replied.

He chuckled and his eyes lit up. "My Grandma used to say the *bank's closed*."

"The bank's closed?"

He nodded. "Yeah. It means there's no kissing tonight, Sweetheart. Of course, that was when they were dating ... just to keep him in line."

Julia giggled at the thought. "Okay. Shake it! I'm dying to

find out the answer."

He rolled it around in his palm and then tossed it on the dashboard. They both leaned forward and looked at the die. It said "Try Again." He tossed it again and frowned when he saw the word "No." Not satisfied with that answer, he tossed it a third time, and the answer was "Maybe."

"I think this die is defective," said John. "We need to return it for one that really works."

"How about if I try?" She scooped up the die with a teasing smile. "Women know how to handle this kind of situation." She rolled it around in the palm of her hands as she said, "You see, Sweetheart. There's a trick to this sort of die. You have to roll it a certain way to get the right answer. Watch."

She grinned mischievously and then said, "I have a sore back from standing all day. My feet hurt and my shoulders ache, not to mention my neck muscles." Julia glanced at John and then asked, "Will my husband give me a good back rub and foot massage when we get home?"

John's eyebrows arched as he watched her take the die from her hand and place it on the dashboard with the word "Definitely" facing up.

Julia smiled. "Now that's how it's done."

"That's cheating!"

"I'm willing to bend the rules a bit if you are."

"Bend the rules?" John asked incredulously as he grabbed her into his arms and held her tight. "I'll do more than rub your feet, you cheating woman!"

With that statement, he began nibbling at her ear, making Julia laugh and squirm in his arms.

When she pushed him away, giggling all the while, John

said, "Well, I guess we ought to go home and take care of those sore feet and aching muscles." He wiggled his eyebrows. "And whatever else needs my attention."

John grinned as he opened the door and climbed out. As he headed for his truck, Julia watched him, trying hard to suppress the laughter bubbling up inside. He was so playful and fun.

Linda Weaver Clarke

Chapter 11

"I don't think we'll have any more problems with Mrs. Evans. I scared the wits out of her tonight. She ran a red light because she was so scared. I believe she'll think twice before pursuing this subject," said the man in white, grinning from ear to ear.

"Are ya sure, Boss?" asked the burly man. He spat black tobacco juice out of the corner of his mouth and then wiped his sweaty forehead with his sleeve. "How do ya know? She's a nosy reporter, ain't she?"

"What woman in her right mind would pursue dead fish and dead cats in exchange for her own life? She received two threatening notes, you stalked her at her place of business, and I jolted her a bit when she left Tuacahn … I had her real scared tonight." Devollyn grinned. "We won't have any more trouble with Mrs. Evans."

Johnson growled his disapproval. His eyes were hard and cold; this man had no compassion whatsoever. His jaw was firm and rigid. He could see that Julia posed a potential threat to them and their work.

He spat more black juice out of the corner of his mouth and said gruffly, "Boss, I think we should've done it my way."

Devollyn furrowed his brow and swore. "If you want to

know where to put the blame, then look at yourself. This whole thing is your fault. With your negative obsession with cats and all, we wouldn't be in this mess in the first place."

"Well, if Fred wouldn't have picked up those mangy cats on the side of the road and started feeding 'em…" Johnson huffed. "They were constantly whining and fussing and wanting our meat. I couldn't stand it no longer. Besides, it weren't my fault. He knows I can't stand cats and that I'm allergic to 'em. That was the last straw. So I took some cyanide from the leach pond and took care of 'em, all right."

"So because of your obsession against cats, we now have a nosey reporter after us."

"It ain't all my fault. That fool you just hired couldn't stand the stench of the leach pond and thought he'd drain it into the creek down yonder. We didn't know that fish were in that stream." Johnson shook his head in disgust. "Like I said, Boss. Let me take care of that lady reporter my way."

Devollyn narrowed his eyes. "You aren't touching the lady. If you lay one hand on her, you're fired."

"You're getting soft, Boss. A pretty face ain't worth all the money we're making."

"That isn't it. If something happens to her, then we'll have the police swarming around the whole area. We wouldn't be able to finish the job. By the way, I heard that Fred found some more gold. He's been working real hard, I understand." When Johnson didn't answer and had a sour-looking face, Devollyn warned once again, "You don't touch her. Got it?"

"Whatever ya say, Boss." Johnson turned on his heels and stormed away, muttering under his breath.

General Steam wasn't a bad place to stay, but it was chilly at nights. They all brought sleeping bags and slept in the large building, but their boss was too soft for that. He brought himself a cot and slept in an adjoining room. He even had a makeshift table where he did his paperwork, jotting down what was found and by whom.

Every evening, they would sit by the fire just outside the main building, converse about the day's work, and eat. But Devollyn seemed above all that. He would eat in town just before toting the crew's food back to camp. Well, Devollyn was the boss, and if Johnson wanted to be paid for the job, he had to obey orders.

Devollyn shook his head in disgust as he watched Johnson stomp away. Why he put up with the man was beyond him. The men he had hired were low-lifes, riff-raff, the scum of the earth, men who would kill for money. And he knew it when he hired them.

Devollyn felt he was above other thieves, and especially above these lowlifes. He was sophisticated with plenty of money, a collector of fine art who listened to classical music and knew important people who could help him climb to the top. His enormous home was in Phoenix, Arizona. He lived the life of luxury and was pleased with himself and his lifestyle.

If this beautiful reporter got in the way, then he would have to do something about it. Money and prestige were priority to him. He could sic his goons on her or just move on and continue his work elsewhere. Blood and killing was not his style, but it was different to his hired miscreants. This was money going down the drain for them if they were chased off, and they would stop at nothing to claim what was coming to them. If Mrs. Evans got in the way, he was afraid what would happen to her.

* * *

It was late, and John and Julia still were not home. A knock came at the door, and April quickly answered it.

"Matthew! I'm so glad you're here," April said with anxiety. "Please come in."

"What's up? Why did you call so late?"

April grabbed his arm and drew him into the house and led him to the sofa. She sat down beside him with concern lacing her eyes.

"I'm sorry I had to get you out at this time of night, but I'm worried about Mom."

"Why?"

"I can't tell you, but I need your help. You mentioned that you're going to meet her in the mountains."

"That's right." Matthew was growing more confused by the minute.

"Will you watch over my mom and dad? Please?"

He laughed, accentuating the dimples in his cheeks. The humor in his eyes was obvious. "Watch over your mom and dad? Now that's a good one."

April straightened and pursed her lips. "I'm serious, Matthew."

He lifted his brow with curiosity and asked, "Why all the mystery, April?"

She placed her hand on his and said, "Please? For me?"

The touch of her hand was gentle, and her smile was genuine, not to mention the effects she was having on him as she laid her warm hand on his. Why did she have to be so appealing, he wondered?

He took a deep breath and answered, "Sure, April. But what do you want me to do without any knowledge whatsoever?"

April shifted in her seat nervously, trying to come up with the right words. She looked into his eyes and said, "I believe my mom is in danger. I want you to be on guard."

Matthew's eyes widened with disbelief. "What?"

"I have proof. I'm not making this up, Matt." Her voice was firm and convincing. "Just trust me and don't ask any questions."

Matthew could not believe his ears. What was she asking? In one breath, she said that her mother was in danger, and in the next, she wouldn't tell him why. This was ridiculous.

With a firm tone, he said, "April, if you know something, why aren't you telling me?"

"Because Mom asked me not to say anything to anyone, and I gave my word."

"What? You say that your mother is in danger, and you gave your word? This is ridiculous. One's word is one thing, but a person's life which is put into jeopardy is another."

April shook her head vigorously. "I can't go back on my word."

"I really think your priorities are mixed up here. Your mother's life is more important than keeping your word."

April stood and put her hands on her hips in a defiant manner and said with a firm voice, "Then if you won't help me, I'll have to go myself and watch them."

April's stubborn attitude was exasperating. She was just like her mother.

Matthew stood and faced her. "April, if your mother is in

danger, then you shouldn't be there either. Now tell me what's going on."

She folded her arms across her waist, then turned around and would not face him. She was frustrated. Her mother said there was nothing to report to the authorities because there was no name on the note. Besides that, she did not want her boss to stop her from doing any more research. April's hands were tied. She had given her word to her mother. The emotion she was feeling was one of fear and frustration, and there was nothing she could do.

Matthew saw the stubborn stance of April… like mother, like daughter. They not only looked a lot alike, but their attitudes were similar. They both were stubborn, pig-headed, and spirited. Not only that, he loved April and would do anything for her. Matthew took her by the shoulders and turned her around so he could speak to her. Talking to someone's back was not his idea of communication. When he turned her around, he saw tears welling up in her eyes, and his heart instantly softened.

"April? What's going on?"

As a tear trickled down her cheek, Matthew pulled her into his arms and held her. The way she burrowed her face into his shoulder and wept touched the inner depths of his heart. He tried to think of soothing words to say, but his mind was blank. Holding her in his arms was like heaven on earth.

Not able to resist, he pressed his lips against the top of her head, hoping that she would not notice. April treated him like a big brother. Matthew knew he had to be patient until she came around to her senses and realized he was the best thing that ever happened to her. He figured no one would ever love April as much as he did.

As he held her, Matthew said tenderly, "April, please tell me what's going on. It breaks my heart to see you like this."

She took a deep breath and said, "Mom received a threatening note to stop pursuing the cyanide incident."

Matthew pulled back instantly and looked into her face. "What? Why would anyone be worried about that? I figured it was just an accidental spilling."

"That's what I thought, too. Mom's run into something bigger than you or I know about."

Matthew stood awhile in thought and then tipped her chin up so he could look into her eyes. "I'll take care of her. There's not much a twenty-four-year-old chemist can do, but I'll keep my eyes and ears open."

"That's all I ask, Matt." She mustered a smile. "You're the best. You've never failed me."

"Yeah," he said quietly. "Remember how you stuck up for me in school when the boys would pick on me and say I was a nerd?"

April smiled. "Yeah, and then you would get as mad as all get out and say that you could fight your own battles."

He chuckled. "That was pride. I didn't want anyone to think I was a wimp. Besides, you were four years younger than me. Can you imagine what that looked like? A feisty twelve year old sticking up for an awkward sixteen year old?"

April suppressed a smile and said humbly, "Sorry about that, but they made me so mad. They were just jealous 'cause you were so smart."

"I doubt that. They were bullies and had to find someone weaker to pick on. It wouldn't have been wise to choose someone bigger than they were."

April grinned. "You've grown quite a bit since then. What are you? Almost six feet tall?"

Matthew cleared his throat indignantly and said, "I beg your pardon. I'm six foot one." He flexed a muscle and grinned. "And I work out at the college gym almost every day, too."

April laughed. "Well, then, in that case, you can fight my battles any day, Matthew." She took his arm and led him to the door. "Please be careful. Remember, I care about you."

Then she rose up on her toes and gave him a peck on the cheek and shoved him out the door.

Matthew blushed and grinned. As April shut the door behind him, he touched the spot that she kissed and said under his breath, "And I care about you, too, April."

Chapter 12

Julia lay awake, listening to the sounds of chirping crickets and the low, soothing sound of her husband's breathing as he slept. She was thinking of the man in white and how he had frightened her that evening. She knew he was the one who had written the threatening notes. It had to be. Why was he trying to stop her investigation?

Julia looked down at her trembling hands, and she became enraged that someone was doing this to her. She was not about to let anyone frighten her from this investigation. She rubbed her hands together in frustration, trying to stop the trembling. When it did not work, she turned on her side and watched her husband's chest rise and fall as he slept on his back. She slid closer and cuddled up to John, wrapping her arm around his waist and curling her leg up, gently resting it on his legs.

That was all it took for John to stir. He felt the softness of her against him and her leg resting on his, so he mumbled sleepily, "Are you still awake?"

"I'm sorry for waking you up. I just can't sleep."

"Because of what happened tonight?"

"Uh-huh."

John could feel that she was uneasy and frightened about

the unknown but still wanted to pursue this assignment. So he turned on his side, slid his arm under her neck, and pulled her closer, giving her the protection and comfort she needed.

Then he said softly, "Julia, you don't have to go ahead with this project. You don't have to out-do Ted."

Julia instantly stiffened and pulled away from him. That was the wrong thing to say, and John immediately wished he could take it back.

Feeling indignant, she said firmly, "I'm not trying to out-do Ted! I can't believe you said that. I've always wanted a good story and now I have it and someone is trying to stop me. Doesn't that prove it must be a good story?"

"Not if it's dangerous. It's just not worth it, Julia. Look at you. You can't sleep, you're scared, and you're a nervous wreck."

"Am not!"

John took her hand in his and could feel a slight trembling. He smiled knowingly and said, "Hmmm, you don't call this scared?"

Julia did not say a word as she jerked her hand away and then stubbornly turned her back towards him.

John knew she was upset, and talking to her back was the last thing he wanted to do. So he rose up, leaned on his elbow, and touched her shoulder. "Sweetheart?"

"I don't want to talk anymore," she huffed. "You're rude and unreasonable."

"Unreasonable?" he said with disbelief.

Who was being unreasonable? That was it. She was impossible to talk to when she was upset. Why did women twist things around when they were mad? Men were so much more rational than women. They didn't let emotion get in the way of a good conversation. But then it was his own fault. Why did he mention Ted in the first place? That was the last person she wanted to discuss. He felt like such a dope.

Hoping to smooth things over, he kissed her cheek and said more humbly, "I'm sorry. I shouldn't have said you were trying to out-do Ted. Forgive me?"

Julia did not say a word, ignoring his honey-coated words.

"I know you'll fret all night long if we don't talk this out. I know you. You won't get a wink of sleep."

Julia rolled on her back and looked up into his face. "Why don't you ever support me? I feel like I have to fight for everything I get."

"I do so support you."

"Only when it's convenient."

"That's not true. I encourage you in a lot of things. You just can't remember because you're mad at me. Remember when you said you wanted to work for the paper but were afraid of neglecting the kids? I believed in you and told you to ask Bill if you could get off work before the kids got home from school. Remember?"

Julia nodded.

"And remember how Ted laughed at you when you were assigned to the Arts Festival last year? I told you to show him up, to delve into the life of an outstanding artist, to find out all you could that would be of interest to the public. Bill was so impressed, and the paper really sold that week."

Julia contemplated his words and bit her lip nervously.

When he took her into his arms, she said softly, "I'm not trying to out-do Ted."

"I know, Sweetheart. You just want a good story. I shouldn't have said that. I was a real dolt."

"I know. I won't disagree with that assessment."

John blinked. "What did you say?"

"You weren't talking sensibly," she said as she cuddled against him. "That's why I forgive you."

He smiled. "Well, at least we agree on one thing. That I didn't have a lick of sense when I mentioned the archenemy."

She laughed and then asked, "So you agree to support me in this?"

John touched his lips to her temple and kissed her lovingly and then whispered, "You're a stubborn woman, Julia, but I'll support you in this. We'll do it together. Okay?"

She looked up into his face and said, "Thank you. That's all I ask, John. I really appreciate it." Then she closed her eyes and relaxed in the comfort of his embrace.

When he felt her relax in his arms and begin to doze off, John could not help but worry about this project of hers. She was determined to see it through. How he loved this woman! From the first day of their marriage, they had an equal relationship. He knew that his wife worked hard, taking care of the children, washing clothes, doing dishes, mowing the lawn, and picking up the house, so he wanted to help in any way possible. Since Julia loved gardening and cleaning, which John was not crazy about, he decided to help with the household duties by cooking. This pleased Julia a great deal.

Every evening, he would experiment on some new recipe or even make one up, if he had a mind to. In fact, he astonished many a houseguest with the cuisine he would share with them, simply because he was so buff and masculine. No one expected it from such a man. He chuckled at the memory of it. Apparently, he didn't fit the mold of a chef.

When he heard Julia breathing evenly, he slid his arm out from under her neck and covered her shoulders with the blanket. As he watched her sleep, with the brightness of the nightlight, he smiled. He kissed her on the cheek and turned over on his side and relaxed. It did not take long until he fell into a sound sleep himself.

***

It was Sunday morning and Julia was feeling better. The threatening notes and Mr. Ponytail didn't seem as frightening today. A good night's sleep made her feel that she could accomplish anything, that she could beat the foe and get her story. On a day like this, she was sure that good would win over evil.

Julia slipped on a black skirt, looked at herself critically in the mirror, and shook her head. She was not in the mood to wear black on this Sunday morning. It was almost springtime, and she was in the mood of a light color.

The flowers in Washington County had started blooming. Oleanders were covered in massive blooms of red, white, and pink, and all the yellow roses were in bud, waiting to burst into blossom.

Julia pulled off the skirt and dropped it to the floor. Next, she grabbed a mauve broomstick skirt and slipped it on. No, she was not in the mood for this style either, so she laid it on top of the reject pile. Then she pulled on a flowered skirt and a lavender knit top to match.

John had been watching with amusement as he put on his suit coat. What was it about women that they had to try on so many different skirts before they made the right choice? All he had to do was take his suit out of the closet and choose a white shirt. Men had it easy. He slowly shook his head.

As Julia scanned the outfit in the mirror, she happened to notice John grinning. "What are you so amused about?"

"You!"

"Me?"

"I don't understand why it takes a third skirt or sometimes the fourth before you make up your mind. Why not the first? In all the years we've been married, I've never seen you choose the first one. Never."

"Well, I can't make up my mind. A woman has to be in the mood of what she wears."

"Mood?"

"Yes, both color and style."

John chuckled. "I'm so grateful to be a man. I don't have to worry about fashion when it comes to a plain old suit for Sunday. Women have to worry about so much."

"What do you mean by so much?"

"Well, there's makeup, fixing your hair, and choosing the right shoes. You stand on one foot, posing like a heron. Then you stand on your other foot and look at the other shoe while trying to keep balance without falling to the floor. Then after trying on several different shoes, you finally choose the first ones you tried on.

"Now, for me, all I do is run a comb through my hair, pull on my suit, and I'm done. When it comes to shoes, I only have one pair for Sunday. I don't need any more shoes than that to be happy."

Just then April walked in with two different styles of shoes on. She stood on one foot and asked, "Mom? Which looks best with this dress?"

At that statement, John burst into laughter.

April glanced at her father and then her mother. "What's come over Dad? Did I miss out on a good joke or something?"

Julia tried hard to suppress her laughter. "Oh, it's nothing."

"Well? What do you think, Mom?" she asked as she dropped her foot to the floor and raised the other one up like a heron standing in water.

Glancing at her husband with a wink, she answered, "Pick the first one you tried on."

John shook his head in amusement and then said, "We'll be late for church if we have to try on any more shoes. Are the girls ready?"

"Yes. They're in the living room waiting."

"Now that's a first," John exclaimed with surprise. "They're usually the ones holding us up. They always forget something just as we walk out the door. If we leave now, it'll give them enough time to run back in the house to get whatever they forgot."

"Dad! That's not nice," April chastised in defense of her sisters.

He just grinned. John knew his daughters quite well. After choosing the right shoes, they all headed toward the car right on time for church.

Just as he was about to lock the door, Faith ran back from the car yelling, "I forgot my scriptures."

She pushed the door open and disappeared.

John shook his head. He was expecting it but was hoping he could lock the door before someone came back. To have a household of daughters was not easy. They were never on time to a meeting, not to mention all the mood swings he had to endure. And the arguments between his daughters were ridiculous. It was usually about someone borrowing the other's clothes without asking. Or if they did ask, they didn't wash it or hang it up after wearing it. Such arguments made his head spin. Between dealing with the mood swings of young women, being consistently late for meetings, and arguments over borrowing clothes, his life was never dull.

Just as Faith walked out of the house, April lunged through the doorway, yelling, "I forgot my purse."

"Your purse?" John asked in amazement. "Why do you need a purse for church? We're not going to town."

"Because it has my breath mints in it, Dad," she said as if he should have known in the first place.

John checked his watch as he stood beside the door waiting, trying to be patient. Just as he blinked his eyes, he saw Julia rush past him and enter the house.

"Julia? What did you forget?"

"I'm chilly. I need a sweater."

John looked toward the car and saw Sharlene sitting all alone in the backseat of the minivan, staring out of the window at him.

John grinned and stretched forth his arm and pointed an accusing finger straight at her and yelled, "Don't you even think about it."

By the time everyone was sitting in the car, five minutes had passed, and they were now fashionably late for church.

Chapter 13

Matthew heaved the barbells up to his chest and then pushed them above his head with a grunt. His biceps pushed against the sleeves of his shirt with each movement, accentuating his muscles. After several reps, he put them away and went to the treadmill. He always made an effort to workout at least three times a week. Being a professor had its toll on a person, both mentally and physically. Working out helped him to relax and get him into shape after sitting at his desk all day.

He stepped on the treadmill, pushed the button, and began walking. As Matthew gradually picked up speed, he thought about April's request to watch out for her mother. What on earth was that girl thinking? How could he help? Her father was going to be there, and John was much tougher than he was. Perhaps she was thinking that two men were better than one. Now that made more sense.

Walking on a treadmill next to him was Matthew's friend and associate at the college. Jeff had been at it for a while and was a little flushed, so he knocked the speed down a notch.

Then Jeff turned to Matthew and said, "I've got a girl I'd like to introduce you to. She's a real looker. She works at this beauty salon. My wife introduced me to her last Saturday when I picked her up and says she's a real catch. She thinks the two of you would get along great. How about this weekend?"

"Naw! Not interested."

Jeff looked at him curiously. "Why not?"

"Because every woman you've set me up with hasn't worked out."

"Worked out? That's because you don't give them a chance. You've never asked one of them out on a second date. Why?"

"They're not my type."

"What do you mean by that? How will you know if you don't go out with her more than once?"

"Well … there's no spark. We don't have anything in common. Not only that, she's either bored with me or I'm bored with her."

Shaking his head with bewilderment, he said, "I don't understand you, Matt."

Jim cleared his throat to get their attention. He had just finished exercising and was resting on a nearby bench, listening to their conversation. He wiped his brow and grinned as he said, "I understand completely."

"What do you mean?" asked Jeff.

"Matt's not interested because none of the ladies measure up. Isn't that right, Matt?"

Matthew turned to him with interest, wondering what sort of knowledge he would expound.

"What do you mean 'measure up'?" asked Jeff.

"You see, the girls you've introduced him to don't have the right name. Now if her name were April Evans, then that would make all the difference in the world."

Matthew stiffened at the mention of April's name. He instantly regretted telling his friend about her. He had confided in him one day when he was completely discouraged, and now his friend had let it out of the bag. He frowned, but Jim grinned all the more.

"You see," continued Jim. "April Evans has qualities that all other women lack. What it is, I don't know. You'll have to ask Matt, but Ken told me she's quite a babe."

At the mention of Ken's name, Matthew furrowed his brow and stared at his friend.

"Ken?" asked Jeff.

"Yeah. He's going to ask her out. He says she's *real hot*."

Matthew pushed the treadmill at a faster speed as his anger began to rise. Real hot? Ken was not good enough for her.

"But," continued Jim, "I don't think Matthew likes the idea too much."

Jeff turned to Matthew and asked, "If this is true, then why aren't you dating her?"

When Matthew ignored his question, Jim said, "I think I might know why. May I give my opinion, Matt?"

Matthew scowled. "Why ask permission? You'd give it anyway."

"True," Jim said with a grin.

"I don't know why I confided in you in the first place," huffed Matthew.

"'Cause we're good friends, Matt. Besides, I can make you feel better just by listening to your problems."

Jeff chuckled. "I think being a psychology professor is going to your head, Jim."

"Well, if you pour your feelings out to someone, then you

feel better, right?"

"Don't know about that. I think it might cause serious damage to pour my soul out to you," Jeff said with a teasing glint in his eyes.

Matthew couldn't believe his ears. His two friends were psychology professors and never agreed on a single thing and now they were discussing his future and whether or not he should pour his feelings out.

Jim looked at Matthew, who was doing his best to ignore them. "Now this is just my opinion, mind you."

"Okay, professor," said Jeff with a smirk. "Why isn't he doing something about it? I'd like to know."

"Well, they grew up together, are good friends, and her family treats him like a son. I believe he doesn't want to rock the boat because April only sees him as a friend."

"Rock the boat?" laughed Jeff. "I don't think you're right. He's afraid of rejection."

"You're wrong. He doesn't want to scare her away," said Jim.

Matthew scowled as he murmured, "Just talk about me as if I weren't even here."

His friends laughed and Jim said, "Personally, I think the problem lies with April, not Matthew. If he gives it some time, then she might come around. You never know about women."

Jeff turned to Matthew and asked, "If that's true, what if it doesn't work out? What if she never sees beyond friendship? Why not explore other waters? Date a little. Get to know other girls during the meantime. Have fun! Perhaps you might find someone much better than April? You never know unless you check out other women."

Matthew huffed, punched the button on the treadmill, and it came to an abrupt stop. He frowned as he stepped off and strode out the door. He was in no mood to talk to his friends about his relationship with April. His friends were beginning to annoy him greatly. Besides, he had to get packed and grab a sleeping bag and some food. He had an errand to do for April. He had made her a promise and Matthew tried to never disappoint her.

* * *

Monday morning, Julia had to go to the office and write up her unfinished article about the Muddy River Relief and put it on Bill's desk. In the meantime, John bought a bunch of groceries for their trip. By the time they finished both projects and got everything packed, it was late afternoon before they left for the mountains. So they decided to take a shortcut through the canyon to save time.

As they passed through Snow Canyon, the red mountains seemed to loom over them. Such beauty was indescribable. Pillars of red rock of every shape and size made Snow Canyon look magnificent. This was Color Country, with roadrunners, horny toads, Gila monsters, coyotes, tarantulas, scorpions, and quail!

Suddenly, Julia cried, "Stop!"

John slammed on the brakes, his heart hammering against his chest. He gasped at the high-pitched sound that had come from his wife's lungs.

He turned to his wife with widened eyes and stammered, "What? What?"

"Quail! See?"

She pointed to a mother, father, and a bunch of babies at the side of the road.

"Yeah?" he said, baffled by her statement.

"I was afraid you were going to run over them. They were about to cross the road, and you didn't even slow down."

John's heart rate had accelerated when she screamed and he was feeling a bit annoyed as he said, "Quail? You yelled because of quail?"

She nodded. "Look!" she said as the quail began to cross the street in front of the truck.

He watched her eyes brighten with excitement. She was enjoying watching this little family and John realized he should have been more patient.

When he heard honking in back of them, John stuck his head out of the window, pointing to the quail as he yelled at the driver, "Stop your blasted honking! Can't you see there's a family of quail here?"

He huffed, looked at his wife, and crossed his arms as he waited for the quail to pass. Julia looked at her husband with complete surprise. It made her smile. After the quail passed, John accelerated, making the tires spin.

After a while, John realized what a dolt he had been and apologized. "Sorry, Julia."

"For what?"

"My outburst."

"Which one?" she asked with a grin. "I think the man behind us was mad."

John looked at her and saw her smiling. He chuckled. Then he said matter-of-factly, "By the way, I brought my revolver. I thought we could do some target shooting. I even bought a bunch of cheap soda cans for targets."

"Targets?"

"Yup. Shake 'em up good, and when you blast 'em, they spurt up like a geyser. Paul and I did it last time we went out. You'll love it. I even got us some cans of shaving cream to shoot at. Just wait and see what happens when you shoot one of those."

He grinned as Julia checked the rearview mirror. Ever since they left home, she had been watching for the Mercedes, but no one was in sight.

Feeling concerned, she asked, "John, if we were ever in danger…" She hesitated. "I mean, if someone was threatening us…" She bit her lip.

"Yeah? Spit it out."

"Well, if you ever had to defend us, would you actually use it?"

"My pistol?" Surprised by her question, he raised his eyebrows. "I'd hope not. Why?"

"Just wondering."

He smiled, and in his best cowboy drawl, he said, "There's a lot of mountain lions out yonder in them hills. An' M'darlin', I'm ready just in case we need to defend ourselves from those varmints… but only as a last resort, of course. Mountain lions are beautiful creatures, but you can't trust 'em."

Her husband was hopeless. She was worried about threatening notes and a reckless Mercedes, and he was joking around. She turned and looked out the window at the scenery. Well, at least she brought her cell phone in case there was an emergency of some kind. That brought a little comfort.

As she thought about how she had stumbled onto the poisoned fish, she was amazed that it had brought on such animosity. She thought that threatening notes and stalking her were a bit much. There had to be something more that she had stumbled on without realizing it. At first, Julia thought she would just take a little excursion up the mountains just to appease Mr. Jones, and perhaps there could be a story of some kind that she could write. She did not expect to find much and was not very hopeful in finding anything since the mountains were so vast. But things were different now.

Sunday night, John had tried to talk her out of going once again, but after remembering what Mr. Jones had said about a Mercedes going into the mountains, she felt it was too much of a coincidence to ignore. Could it be the same Mercedes that tried to push her off the road?

She looked at John and said, "Matthew will be meeting us tomorrow morning to get some samples to take back to the lab, but he'll only stay for a couple hours and then head back."

John smiled. "Good. That way we can have the rest of the day to ourselves. We deserve it. Both of us have been working way too hard."

They approached a small, black, dome-shaped volcanic cinder cone. There were several in the area that made for interesting scenery. A gigantic volcano located in Pine Valley had been inactive for thousands of years and had created these rugged features. The mountainous volcano was now a most beautiful state park and community.

After a while, John turned toward Gunlock. The town was still closed off, but the road that led into the mountains toward General Steam was still open. They drove down a steep winding hill and then headed toward the mountains on a dusty, bumpy dirt road.

As the truck climbed higher and higher, Julia noticed how gorgeous the mountains were, greener than she had ever seen because of all the rain. It was March and spring was in the air! New leaves were budding on every tree and shrub. In the background were rolling desert hills and rugged mountains all around them. The only trees visible were fifteen to twenty foot junipers. There were scrub oak, desert vines hanging from trees, and fresh-smelling sagebrush, which was an awesome sight to behold. In every direction, there was such beautiful, romantic scenery.

The bumpy, winding road went over one hill after another, which made for slow driving, about twenty-five miles per hour.

Just as they came upon a small clearing surrounded by cottonwood trees, Julia pointed. "There! This is perfect. We can get some samples from that creek tomorrow morning when Matthew arrives."

John did as he was told, just as a Hummer passed by. Julia looked at the driver and inwardly gasped. It was the same man that had frightened her in the parking lot. The only fear she had now was whether or not he had seen her as he passed. Wherever that Hummer was heading was the answer to her story. She knew that much.

After taking samples from the streams, they would drive over the mountain the long way home. Perhaps they might run into that yellow Hummer on the way.

John slowly pulled his truck down a small hill into the flat area. It was a lovely spot, with a bubbling creek nearby and tall cottonwood trees, making good shade for camping.

Julia opened the door and breathed in the fresh mountain

air. When the truck rubbed against the sagebrush, disturbing the delicate leaves, it left a deliciously pleasant odor in the air. She stretched and looked around. She could hear the sound of the river in the distance and the chirping of birds in nearby trees. They seemed to be singing to one another, as if echoing what the other had announced and spreading the news abroad.

Julia walked to the back of the truck where John was taking out their belongings to set up camp. He glanced at his wife and smiled. She was such a good sport. He knew the ground was not that comfortable since they had turned forty, as if their bodies had changed overnight. But this was important to her, and she did not complain. In fact, he had packed extra padding for Julia as a surprise so the ground would not feel so hard.

As John pulled the tent out of the truck, he asked, "Hungry?"

Julia took a deep breath and let it out slowly. "Starving."

When she heard the river in the background, she could hardly wait to check it out. What would she find? Would there be any signs of poisoning? Was someone polluting the water? If so, then it should be stopped. The environment had to be protected.

Chapter 14

"What do you think, Julia? This spot is as good as any, don't you think?" John said as he dropped the tent to the ground.

As he put up the tent, Julia cleared a spot for the fire pit, putting rocks around an area to control the fire. Then she set up the folding table and chairs near the fireplace, leaving the food in the back of the truck until they needed it.

When a slight breeze touched Julia's cheeks, she breathed in the fresh air and realized how much she had missed camping. It was so lovely here. Birds were twittering love songs, and the sound of nature was everywhere. Deep green junipers added to the beauty of this desert land, with cottonwood trees lining the creek.

Feeling curious, she strolled toward the river. Julia ducked under a few low-hanging cottonwood branches that swayed in the gentle breeze. She worked her way through the brush and growth until she came upon the creek. She saw a squirrel near the stream, but it scampered away when it heard her coming. Not too far downstream was a young mule deer drinking water. When it lifted its head and saw her in the distance, it immediately bolted away into the desert. When she looked at the slow-moving river, she saw water-skitters skimming the river in a spot that was calm.

There were no signs of death around here. As she searched the banks, Julia found nothing that would convince her of a spillage. The creek was clear and peaceful. Perhaps the excess water from the mountains during the flooding had flushed away any signs of cyanide and she would never find a story up here after all. But what about the soil? There might be signs left there. And how about the seedy-looking men that Mr. Jones had warned her about? This was so mysterious. They must be doing something secretive, simply because of their threats.

Across from the creek was a solid rock wall, giving the place a special privacy from the rest of the desert. This area was greener than most. It had willows growing around it, and lush vines were hanging over nearby shrubs and rocks. There was speckled gray sand beside the creek that seemed so inviting to Julia. She decided to slip her shoes off and feel the cool sand between her toes. She saw a flat boulder near the creek and sat down to enjoy the quiet solitude of the afternoon. There was serenity here that she enjoyed, which brought a feeling of contentment to her soul.

As Julia sat, listening to nature, she heard a rustling sound and turned to find a couple of baby cottontail rabbits. They had soft, white, fluffy tails hugging their backsides, which made them look absolutely adorable. She quietly watched them for a few seconds. They must have felt her presence because they looked up and fear overtook them. They instantly scampered away, bumping and colliding into each other as they disappeared into a hole in the ground.

Julia laughed. It was quite a sight. She knelt down and cupped her hands in the clear, fresh water and realized it was not killing the wild life in the area. Those were healthy baby rabbits.

She pulled a hanky from her pocket, dipped it in the water, and dabbed her face and neck, wiping the dust from her skin. It felt so refreshing.

As Julia rested the hanky against her cheek, she sensed that eyes were upon her. She slowly scanned the surrounding area, wondering what she was looking for. Something seemed out of sync with the sound of nature. Silence. That was it. It had become silent all of a sudden. The birds had stopped chirping. She heard a slight movement in the woods and sensed it was not an animal hiding among the trees. She could feel it inside. A cold chill swept down her spine and she shivered. Was it just her imagination?

Julia had an eerie feeling inside as she remembered the threatening notes, the man in the Mercedes, and the seedy-looking man who had passed them on the road.

Behind her, she heard the crack of a twig and she jumped out of her skin. Julia quickly turned around, her face draining of its color as she saw her husband walking toward her.

"Hey! Did you find anything?"

"No," she said as she breathed a sigh of relief. She cautiously scanned the woods once again and then she looked at John, feeling uneasy. "Let's go back to camp. I'm hungry. We haven't had supper and it's getting late."

"Sounds good to me."

John quickly got the fire started while Julia pulled out two small cans of juice, some hot dogs, and a bag of chips. He grabbed two rods from the truck and pulled them to full length. Then he stuck a hot dog on the end of his, sat down on a folding chair, and dangled it over the fire.

"Come on, Julia. The fire's perfect."

She laughed and picked up her camera and said, "I've just got to get a picture of this. Where did you find those rods?"

"Paul and I found them on our last camping trip."

He looked at the camera with a goofy smile as he held his rod and hot dog in hand. After clicking the photo, Julia grabbed a hot dog and stuck it on the end of the rod and sat beside her husband.

Without thinking, she asked, "What do you suppose the children are doing now?"

John laughed. "Our children are so much a part of our lives that we can't even have quiet time together without thinking about them."

Julia smiled. "Sorry. Couldn't help it."

"I know. It's the motherly instinct in you."

She slid her chair next to his, put her hand through the crook of his arm, and leaned her head on his shoulder and sighed.

John felt something was wrong. He took the rod from her hand and held it over the fire. "What's wrong, Julia?"

"Nothing."

"Hey, I know you better than that."

"What if this is all a wild goose chase like Ted insinuated? What if it really is an accidental spilling and those seedy-looking men that Mr. Jones told me about are afraid of getting into trouble and that's all."

John smiled. "Julia, it won't be the end of the world if it is. I wouldn't worry so much. Besides, if it comes to nothing, I've got something for you to work on that would be more exciting than dead fish and stinky cats."

Julia's head lifted from his shoulder, and she looked into his eyes. "What?"

"Something big."

"Something big? What are you talking about?"

John took a deep breath and let it out slowly, trying to figure out how to tell her that he had not been completely honest with her. Here he had been lecturing her about honesty, and he hadn't been so honest himself.

"Julia, I've been feeling guilty about something. You know when I got after you about keeping secrets from me?"

She nodded.

"Well, I shouldn't have been so hard on you, because I'm just as guilty."

Julia sat up straight. "What do you mean?"

"Well, I was worried you would put yourself in danger if you found out what I know."

"Yes, I'm listening."

"Julia, please don't be angry with me, all right?"

She narrowed her eyes and said in a cautious manner, "Go on."

"You see..." He hesitated, trying to find the right words. "The archaeologists haven't returned, and there's been digging going on at the sites. In fact, Paul thinks a whole new pueblo has been found."

"What are you trying to tell me?"

He licked his dry lips and plunged in. "It's unlawful digging, pirating, thievery, looting. Now, do you understand what I'm saying, Julia?"

She nodded, her large hazel eyes staring into his. She was hurt ... and she was hurt deeply. John hid something from her because he didn't trust her. How could he do this to her?

This would be the biggest story ever. By the time the archaeologists were ready to give permission to let the story out, Ted would have been assigned to it. That's just the way the system worked.

John could see the hurt in her eyes, and he felt terrible. "Julia, please forgive me. I was just worried about you. That's all. I just wanted to protect you."

Julia hopped up and strode toward the tent.

"Julia? Where are you going?"

"Mother Nature is calling," she said irritably, not wanting to speak to him anymore. What he had done was selfish, simply because he didn't trust her.

John had set up a toilet among some bushes not far from camp. She grabbed a small bag of wet wipes from the tent, stuffed them in her pocket, and disappeared into the woods where she could be alone and think. Tears welled up in her eyes, and she angrily wiped them away with the back of her hand. She knew her husband loved her, and that was why he wanted to protect her. As she thought about the situation, she tried to understand the reasoning behind it. If she found out that her husband might be in danger, would she do the same thing?

Julia shook her head. No, she would give him a chance to prove himself. She would trust him.

After answering the call of nature, she headed back. As she walked toward camp, she remembered the feeling of being watched at the river, wondering if it had been her imagination. The thought of being watched gave her an uncomfortable feeling. For someone to know her every move was disconcerting.

Julia pushed the irrational thoughts out of her mind. She

was being ridiculous. No one knew she was there because no one followed her and she knew that for sure. She had constantly watched the roads. She shook the idea out of her mind and continued on her way.

Julia was just a few yards from camp when she heard the most piercing, blood-curdling sound she had ever heard in her life. The sound of a wild animal in the distance startled her beyond words. Julia's heart jumped. Her hands trembled and her legs became weak. To add to her fears, she absolutely hated the dark.

When she heard another high-pitched screech and a snarling sound, it frightened her so badly that she screamed and darted for camp. Just as she got beyond the trees, she stumbled and tripped over a branch and landed right into John's arms.

He had bolted from his seat at the sound of her screaming. When she came running from the woods, he saw her stumble and dashed toward her just in the nick of time.

"Whoa, lady! What's gotten into you, lately? You're as nervous as a…"

"Did you hear that, John?"

"The mountain lion?" John asked as he helped her to her feet. "Sure, but it's not even close. There's nothing to worry about. It was probably catching its dinner." John looked down into her eyes and saw the frightened look. "Hey, you were scared, weren't you?"

John put his arm around her trembling shoulders and led her to the fire pit as he said, "I finished cooking your hot dog and put it in a bun with relish. I put carrots, pickles, and chips on your plate, too. Want some juice?"

Seeing the softness in his eyes, Julia knew that fixing her

meal was his way of saying he was sorry. He often did kind gestures like this to make up for an argument and she always appreciated it. She sat down on the folding chair, staring into the blazing fire and chastising herself for being so edgy.

Seeing Julia's nervousness, John tried to calm her down. "Hey, don't be so hard on yourself. You didn't know the mountain lion wouldn't come this way."

Julia bit her lip. Then looking at her husband, she asked, "Have you ever been in a situation where you had to defend yourself from a wild animal?"

"No." John took her hand and squeezed it lovingly. "Don't worry. Mountain lions don't like to come around humans. " He grinned. "And if one does, I'll protect you."

"What's wrong with me?" She puffed out a breath of air. "There was no reason to get so frightened, was there? Isn't that right? Huh?"

He chuckled, knowing she was asking for reassurance. "I'll set up the sleeping bags while you finish your food."

Julia nodded absently as she took a bite of her hot dog. It hit the spot. Why did hot dogs taste so delicious over a fire compared to a stove? By the time Julia finished, she felt better and had settled down. For some reason, food had a tendency to relax one's nerves.

As she quickly undressed in the dark, she pulled on some flannel pajamas, shivering and shuddering all the while. Getting undressed in the cold was a part of camping she had never really enjoyed. As fast as she could, she slipped into their full-sized sleeping bag and into the arms of her husband. Julia snuggled up close, hoping to feel his warmth as soon as possible.

He chuckled at her cuddling and snuggling. "Hey, you

came prepared."

"What?"

"Flannel pajamas."

Julia grinned. "It's cold up here. They're warm."

"I wouldn't worry about that, M'darlin'. I'm in charge of keeping you warm, protecting you from varmints and such."

Julia smiled. "Like mountain lions?"

"You bet!" He pulled her close and asked mysteriously, "Have you heard about the three sisters that lived together, ages ninety-two, ninety-four, and ninety-six?"

"No. What about them?"

"Let me tell ya," said John with a grin, hoping to bring some laughter into the tent. "Well, the ninety-six year old filled her bathtub and stepped in and then said, 'Wait a minute. Was I getting in or getting out?' The ninety-four year old heard her and said, 'I'll come upstairs and see.' She got halfway up the stairs and said, 'Wait a minute. Was I going up or going down?' The ninety-two year old, sitting at the kitchen table and having a cup of tea, heard them both. 'Boy, I sure hope I don't get that bad when I'm their age. Knock on wood,' she said as she knocked on the table. Then she called out, 'Just a minute and I'll come help you both as soon as I find out who's at the door.'"

Julia burst into uncontrollable laughter.

Watching her jovial attitude, John grinned and wished he could remember another joke to tell her. She was so much fun. After a bit of playful bantering, teasing, and a few romantic, luscious kisses, they finally settled down for a good night's sleep. Within minutes, she began to doze.

She had had a big day and was weary. Julia's nerves were frayed. Her heart had flipped over a few times after the mountain lion episode. And to add to her stress, she thought she was being watched. What more could possibly happen to her?

Chapter 15

The sun was up, the air was chilly, and the birds were chirping their cheery message of the day. John was awake and watching Julia sleep peacefully. He realized that she was quite uptight yesterday, and he was glad she was sleeping soundly. He smiled and tenderly ran a finger over the contours of her face. His heart swelled within him, feeling an overwhelming love for the woman that lay beside him. She was simply lovely, even in her sleep. How he adored her! In many ways, she was a challenge to him because of her stubbornness. And in other ways, she was a complete jewel, because she was so patient with his weaknesses.

John quietly slipped out of the sleeping bag and pulled on his clothes. As he opened the flap of the tent, he heard a rattling noise, and he instantly froze when he saw the snake in front him. It was in a tight circle, rattling its gray tail. The snake was huge and in a bad mood. No one was going to leave that tent.

As John eyed the rattler, he wondered why it was guarding his tent. Usually snakes hid in the rocky ground. This was unusual. Besides that, it was upset and ready to strike and John could not figure out why, especially because he had done nothing to provoke it.

He watched for a few seconds, wondering if he should just wait until it left or if the rattler was as stubborn as it looked. The only thing to do was to wait it out. If he fired a shot at it, then Julia would be frightened out of her wits. He turned and watched her sleeping peacefully. It was not worth it. He would wait.

After a while, he heard a rustling sound and peeked outside and the rattler was slithering away. Perhaps it had been cold last night and found a nice warm place to sleep. After it was safe, John quickly slipped out of the tent and grabbed a long, slender stick. He quickly slid the stick under the snake before it escaped, carried it to the river, dropped it in, and watched it float downstream. He was worried Julia might run into it out in the woods.

Should he mention this episode to her? As he thought about it, why say anything? He had taken care of the snake and it was gone. Julia didn't need to worry about another so-called varmint.

While he was at the river, John washed up and felt more presentable for the day. He ran a hand across the stubble on his face and decided that it would be better to rough it. He was not in the mood to shave.

When he returned, he found Julia stepping unsteadily out of the tent in her flannel pajamas. She raised her arms above her head and stretched the sore muscles in her body.

"Hey, sleepyhead! It's about time you woke up," John said with a grin as he noticed her unsteady movements. "Get freshened up while I get breakfast ready. You'll feel better in no time. If the cold mountain water doesn't revive you, nothing will. Take my word for it. Personally, I believe this freezing water would wake the dead."

Julia sleepily grabbed a brush, a washcloth, a towel, and the biodegradable liquid soap. Then she put on her robe and slipped on her tennis shoes. John chuckled as he watched her walk toward the river. Julia was always slow and clumsy in the morning. When she would wake up, she always seemed to be poorly coordinated. It was as if her body had slept so soundly that it could not get going without a little help. He remembered when she once rammed into the side of the bedroom door when she got up in the night.

John yelled out, "Hey, don't fall in the river."

He chuckled and then began preparing their breakfast. He had packed a small Dutch oven with bacon and eggs along with orange juice. First thing, he would start a fire to warm the atmosphere.

Julia slowly walked toward the river, trying to get both her equilibrium and wits about her. After she arrived, she sat beside the river and groaned. She had slept soundly, but the ground felt harder than it was the last time they camped with the girls.

Julia pushed her sleeves up and undid a few buttons at her neck. Then she dipped the washcloth in the icy water and wrung it out. She squirted soap on it and washed her face and neck. As she placed the rag on her warm skin, she shivered. Why was she torturing herself so early in the morning, she wondered?

She dipped the cloth in the water once again, wrung it out, and quickly rinsed herself off, quivering and shaking once again. The cold water had definitely awakened her senses. She quickly patted her face and neck with the towel, taking a few deep breaths.

Feeling refreshed, Julia got to her feet. What was it about

mountain spring water that made one cringe from the coldness and at the same time feel fresh and alive?

As she buttoned her pajama top, Julia heard the crack of a twig just beyond a few tall bushes not far from where she stood. She turned toward the sound and searched the area and saw nothing. An overwhelming feeling of apprehension hit her suddenly. It was the same feeling she had yesterday. Was someone watching her, or was she being paranoid because of the threatening notes? Was she letting her imagination get away with her? Mr. Ponytail could not have known where she was. How could he?

It was probably another cottontail like yesterday. They were absolutely delightful. Julia grabbed her belongings and headed toward the bushes to check out the noise. She had to know the truth or it would eat at her all day.

Julia checked the ground for tracks as she walked along. There was nothing but the prints of squirrels and rabbits. Feeling relieved, she laughed at herself for being so paranoid.

Just as she turned to leave, she stumbled and dropped her bottle of soap. It bounced off a log, rolled down an incline, and landed right in the mud. What awful luck!

She walked toward it, stooped down to pick it up, and beside the bottle was a set of large footprints. She could see they were fresh. A cold chill ran down her spine. Someone had actually been here after all. Had he observed everything she was doing?

Yesterday, her feelings of being watched were not her imagination after all. The movement she had sensed in the woods was real. What seemed to be out of sync with nature was not in her mind.

Should she tell her husband, and would he insist on

leaving? She had promised to be honest with him and not keep anything from him. Julia knew she had to keep that promise. Feeling a growing sense of uneasiness, she immediately rushed for camp, not knowing what she would say to John. But she did realize one thing; she had to tell the truth. She could not keep this from her husband.

When she arrived, Matthew was sitting and chatting with John. As she thought about it, she decided to wait and talk about this later when Matthew wasn't around. She had invited him to take samples of water and soil, hoping to find some residue of cyanide along the stream. That was before the Mercedes rammed her on Saturday.

After that incident, Julia had adamantly told him that she didn't need him any longer, and she could bring the samples back with her. But he stubbornly insisted that he had to and then hung up the phone, ending all conversation. She smiled at how much he wanted to help. There was something about Matthew that wormed his way into her heart. He was like the son she never had.

When Matthew saw Julia approach in her old baggy robe and pajamas, he whistled and said, "Hey! That's a nice outfit, Julia."

She laughed. "Thanks. I knew you were coming, so I decided to put on my best attire. Did you have a tough time finding us?"

"Naw! I looked for the little sign you left on the side of the road. You know, rocks piled up a few layers next to the turnoff."

"Great! Did you bring everything you need?"

"Yup. Sure did."

"Good. I'll be dressed in no time and then we'll get

started."

"Hey, you!" John called out. "Not until you eat a bite of breakfast."

Julia smiled. "That, too," she said as she disappeared into the tent.

As she dressed, she told herself that she would tell John about the footprints later when they were alone. As for now, they were going to get samples along the creek and then head upstream, searching for more evidence.

As she dressed, John yelled out to her, "I'm filling our packs full of food. That way we can stay out as long as we need to."

Chapter 16

Matthew and Julia took off along the river, while John decided to explore the countryside. As they hiked upstream, taking samples of water and anything that looked suspicious, they talked. Matthew was able to talk to Julia easily. She was like a second mother to him. It was Julia who encouraged him to make something of himself. She told him to go to college when he felt discouraged. He had come from a broken home and had low self-esteem. At the age of ten, Julia befriended him and made him feel important. He felt more at home with the Evans family than at his own.

They were neighbors, but when Matthew's family life fell apart, Julia had seen the need to comfort him and invite him over to eat or watch a movie with the family. That was when he was a kid, and he found himself at their home more than his own. He grew up with the girls and knew they had accepted him as a family member. That made him feel good, since he was an only child.

Julia understood his mood swings and knew when he needed to talk. When he was blue or depressed about his life, she would sit him down on the sofa, tell the girls to go to bed, and then have a heart-to-heart talk with him. She would tell him how valuable he was and to not get discouraged. Then she would take him in her arms and hold him as he wept. Julia wondered why the family fell apart. It was so hard on children.

After he went home, she would go to her bedroom and tell her husband what Matthew had said. Tears would stream down her cheeks as she told him every detail. And then she would ask, "Why do children have to be in the middle? Why can't their parents try harder?"

John listened and said nothing, his heart going out to Matthew. But that wasn't all. When he lacked for money, Julia would push some bills in his pocket. When he refused, she would shake her finger and say, "You're one of us. Remember that!"

Matthew now needed her wisdom. He decided to have a heart-to-heart talk with Julia once again. He had always called her by her first name, even though she was like his mother. He never knew why, but it came easy to him. Perhaps it was because she was his friend and treated him as such. Besides, calling her Mrs. Evans was too formal.

Matthew realized that he needed to get up his courage to say what was on his mind. He stuck his hands in his pockets and kicked at a rock, making it fly toward the water's edge.

Taking a deep breath, he said, "Can I bend your ear for a moment?"

"Of course. Since when do you need to ask?"

He smiled. "You were the first one who encouraged me to follow my dreams. And because of you, I went to college and now I'm doing what I've always wanted to."

"I'm glad, Matthew. I knew you had great potential. You were always a bright young man, and I knew you could do it."

"Thanks. But now I have another problem, something I

can't figure out on my own."

"What can I do to help?"

"Well, it's April."

"April's a problem?" Julia said with a laugh. "She's the easy-going one. Now if you had said the twins, I would understand. Has she teased you mercilessly?"

"I wish it was only that."

Glancing at Matthew, she asked, "What is it?"

"Well, she's been my friend ever since we were kids. But that's all she wants to be ... my friend. And nothing else."

Julia stopped in her tracks and looked at him thoughtfully. She could always tell what he was thinking through his eyes... *the window to his soul*. His eyes told what was in his heart.

As she gazed at him, it took her aback. What she saw was a young man in love. Julia had always known that he would make some lucky woman very happy. But was that young woman her very own daughter?

Julia's eyes softened as she asked, "Are you in love, Matthew?"

He hesitated for a moment and then answered, "Yes."

"With April?"

Matthew nodded. "But she'll have nothing to do with me, if you know what I mean."

"Hmmm." She thought for a moment, looking toward the mountains. "I'm not sure what advice to give you, Matthew. Maybe just give her time. She's not ready for marriage. She wants to be a master potter, as you well know."

"Yes, I know. I've seen her works. They're excellent."

Julia nodded as she said tenderly, "Matthew, just go slow and she'll come around. One never pushes for a relationship, especially with April. She's one obstinate young lady and doesn't like to be pushed. It has to come naturally with her. Take April to the movies and concerts only as a friend, and it won't take long for her to see where your heart lies."

Matthew nodded and gave a grim smile. "Thanks."

"Don't give up, all right? Any young woman would be lucky to have you."

He smiled shyly from her compliment. "Okay. And I don't give up easily. I can be just as stubborn as April."

Julia laughed at his determined attitude. "Personally, I'd like you in the family. But my advice is to go slow."

"Thanks. I'll do that."

Not too far off, they heard the crunching of twigs and leaves behind them and turned around. John had caught up to them and gave a little wave. He knew they would be following the river upstream, so all he had to do was follow it.

As he approached, he said, "Hey, you two! Why so serious?"

Julia smiled. "O-o-oh, just talking. That's all. Where have you been?"

John put his arm around Julia's shoulder and said in an excited tone, "I was hiking along the side of the mountain and found a mysterious cave."

"You what?"

His eyes brightened with excitement. "Yeah! Want to see it?"

Julia grinned when she saw his enthusiasm. "Why not? We've got what we need. We're done." She turned to Matthew and said, "Then I insist that you go home afterwards, all right?"

Matthew cleared his throat with discomfort and said, "I

brought my sleeping bag with me. I've decided to stay until morning."

"No, Matthew," she said, shaking her head. "You really don't have to."

"Yes, I do. It's for April," he said in no uncertain terms. Then he turned to John and smiled. "Now I'd like to see this mysterious cave of yours."

Julia knew that Matthew had made up his mind, and there was nothing she could say or do to persuade him to leave. So she nodded and followed the two men toward the mountain.

It took some time to get to the cave. The hike was long and steep, but the day was pleasant enough, not too hot and not too chilly. The sun was shining, warming their shoulders as they hiked. The cave was just below the rugged portion of the mountain, and the entrance was hidden from view by a bunch of cedar trees. The opening to the cave had wooden supports around the sides and top with an inscription etched on one of the slabs. It read, "Constructed 1905." The wood was dark and looked old and crumbly, which worried Julia.

John pointed to it and said, "Be careful. Don't touch the wood. I don't know how much pressure it can take. The other supports inside seem sturdier though, not as worn by the weather. The tunnel goes back quite a ways."

Julia hesitated.

"It's safe. I already checked it out."

John pulled out his mini-flashlight from his pack, turned it on and then motioned for them to follow. They went a few yards before the tunnel made some twists and turns.

"I figure this was a hermit's home once upon a time or

perhaps an outlaw's hideout. Or maybe some of the workers at the mining community made it and stored stuff here. Who knows?"

"Mining community?"

"Yup. Better known as General Steam."

Julia nodded. "How old is General Steam, anyway?"

"Hmmm, I think it was around the early 1900s when they began mining up here. Some people brought their families with them, and they even built several homes and planted some fruit trees. I'll have to show you, perhaps tomorrow morning before we leave. It's getting too late to show you today."

"I've heard a lot about it. I'd like to see it. Thanks."

After walking a few more yards, they entered a large cavity. In one corner was a pile of old bones from dead animals. Caves provided shelter for a variety of animals to either escape the harsh winter weather or the heat of the summer months. Against the wall at the opposite end of the cave were a couple of old chairs, a rickety table, and a small wooden chest with rusty hinges.

John smiled mischievously. "Hmmm, a treasure chest!" he said in his most mysterious voice. "What do you think, Julia? Do you think there's some valuable treasure inside? Maybe jewels or Spanish doubloons? Did you know the famous Spanish trail runs not too far from here?"

"No, I didn't." Curiosity got to Julia and she said, "Open it, John."

He pulled a handkerchief from his pocket and dusted off the top of the chest and then slowly creaked open the rounded lid. The anticipation was great as he opened it and everyone leaned forward to look inside. There was a rusty hammer, old rusted nails, a crumpled up gunnysack, and a discolored candle sitting on a copper stand.

Julia picked up the copper stand and admired it. She placed it on the table and smiled. "What do you think? It matches the décor in the room."

John took a look and chuckled. "Yup, it sure does." Then he picked up the gunnysack and said speculatively, "Hmmm, perhaps this contains golden coins left here by some outlaws like Butch Cassidy and the Wild Bunch."

Julia laughed. "Yeah, sure, John. I think you've been watching too many cowboy movies lately."

John slipped his hand in the sack and wiggled his fingers around playfully as if searching for treasure. He stopped and his eyes widened in surprise as he looked at Matthew and Julia.

"There's something inside here."

His fingers wrapped around a bunch of paper, and he slowly pulled out a handful. He opened his hand and in his palm was a wad of crumpled money mingled with sandy dust. Julia's mouth dropped open. Matthew's eyes widened.

John blew the dust off the money and said, "Well, well... what do we have here? Perhaps a band of outlaws stuffed their money in these old sacks after robbing a bank."

"Do you think so?" asked Matthew.

"Yup. Could've been Butch Cassidy. He didn't live very far from here, you know. He was born and raised in southern Utah."

Julia knelt down beside John and looked at the money, her eyes as wide as saucers. "How much is there, John?"

He peeked inside the sack and about choked. "Oh, it looks like a few thousand dollars. What do you think we should do with it?"

Matthew was dumbfounded and unsure what to say.

John rubbed his chin thoughtfully. "Do you think we should report it or just keep it? The bank probably doesn't even exist any longer. Besides that, we don't even know whether it was stolen or not. What do you say?"

Julia stared at the crumpled money in disbelief and then got a questioning look in her eyes. "Wait a minute. There's something wrong here." Julia looked up at her husband. "Shine your light on the money, John."

He did as he was told.

Julia frowned as she took a crumpled bill from his hand. "Why isn't this money all yellowed with age?"

She unfolded it and looked at every detail closely. John was trying so hard to suppress his laughter as she inspected the bill.

After a few moments, she furrowed her brow and narrowed her eyes as she looked at her scoundrel of a husband.

"What?" he asked innocently.

"2005? The year is 2005, John!"

The corners of John's mouth began to quiver as he tried to stifle a chuckle. Only a reporter's eyes would recognize a phony bill, and John was proud of her. When she stared at him with those big hazel eyes, he was unable to hold it back any longer and he burst into a fit of laughter. It did not take long until his chest rose and fell uncontrollably as he guffawed, slapping his leg at the same time. He had got her. And he had got her good. It was one of the best jokes he had created in a long time.

Julia slugged him in the shoulder, causing more laughter

to erupt. "You tricked us!"

Matthew chuckled, "You really fooled me. That was a good one, John. Did you see Julia's face? You almost had her."

Julia picked up the sack and looked inside. It was stuffed with more gunnysacks to give it a full look. He had gone to a great deal of work to deceive them. What a rotten trick! Watching them laugh, she felt embarrassed that she had been taken in so easily.

As Julia stood, she swung the gunnysack into John's body and said, "Just laugh it up, you hyenas! One of these days you'll get yours, John Evans. Just you wait. I'll get you one of these days when you're unaware."

John burst into another fit of laughter once again as she tried to suppress a smile. What a scoundrel!

* * *

The stars were shining brightly, and everyone was sitting around the campfire when a sound was heard in the distance. Everyone's ears perked up as they listened. Julia's eyes widened as she looked anxiously toward her husband and whispered, "Did you hear that?"

John nodded as he pursed his lips together, as if thinking deeply about the strange sound he had heard.

"What do you think it is?"

He whispered, "Not sure, Julia."

"Someone's walking around out there, John. I just know it."

"Well, I don't think it's our little friendly mountain lion this time."

"What do you think we should do?"

He shrugged. "Don't know." Then he rose to his feet and whispered, "I'll be back."

Julia immediately grabbed his shirtsleeve and held on tight, trying to hide the instant rush of fear that she felt deep inside.

"You're not going out there, John," she demanded.

He looked at her with concern and patted her hand. "Julia, if you're right, then whoever it is shouldn't be spying on us, especially after what you told me about those footprints in the mud. Whoever is spying on my wife is going to get his head knocked off."

"About those footprints ... maybe he was just passing through," she said, knowing it sounded lame.

John narrowed his eyes and said with a little impatience, "Julia, you know better than that."

"I know. But I don't want you going out there."

John pried her hand loose from the firm grip on his shirt, grabbed a long stick near the fire, and stood.

Then he turned to Matthew and said firmly, "Stay here and watch over Julia. I'll be back in five minutes."

"Not a minute later?" asked Julia with concern.

John nodded, and without another word, he strode off through the cottonwood trees and bushes.

Matthew wrapped his arm around Julia's shoulder to console her. "It's okay. Don't worry. He'll be back."

Julia looked at Matthew as she anxiously bit her lower lip. "Matthew? Tell me when five minutes are up."

After a minute had passed, she began pacing. Standing still was nerve racking, to say the least. After a few more minutes, she stopped and looked into the woods and shook her head with frustration.

"How long has it been?"

Matthew checked his watch by the glow of the fire. "About three minutes."

Julia was stricken with fear. Why did her husband have to go out in the dark just like some mystery novel and find out what the sound was? This was the very thing she had made fun of in suspense movies, and now John had done it. Julia tried to fight the increasing panic rising within her as she continued pacing back and forth.

After a couple of minutes, Matthew said with a grin, "You're going to wear a low spot in the ground."

Julia tried to force a smile as she asked, "How long has it been?"

"Two minutes from the last time you asked."

"It's been five minutes. I shouldn't have allowed him to go out there, Matthew."

"Could you have stopped him?"

Julia shook her head and stared into the dancing flames. A few minutes later, John came walking back with his tiny flashlight in one hand and the long stick in the other. He turned it off and stuffed it in his pocket.

"You're late," she said accusingly.

John grinned with amusement. "Sorry about that."

Matthew looked at him curiously and asked, "Well? Did you find something?"

"Sure did. There was someone out there. I examined the ground, and there were footprints. Looks like fresh ones, too." He turned to his wife as he tossed the stick into the bonfire. "I've been doing some thinking about this, Julia. I don't think he's here to harm us, or he would have when we first arrived. I've got a hunch that whoever it is must be watching us to see if we're any threat to him."

Matthew's eyes widened. "Did you say threat?"

John nodded and then turned to his wife. "What would they want with you, Julia? You have done nothing to earn this sort of attention."

"Except write an article in the paper," she said meekly.

John sat down on a folding chair and shook his head in dismay. "Yeah, about dead fish and cats. Why? It just doesn't make sense."

Matthew was speechless.

John huffed. "We're heading back home tomorrow morning, Julia."

When he looked at her, she didn't offer any rebuttal. Good! Thank heaven for little miracles. He was afraid that the "reporter" side of her would baulk.

After a while, he got to his feet and said, "It's late and I'm tired. I'm hitting the sack."

Julia sat down and gazed into the orange flames, biting her lip and wondering what was going on.

"Hey, you!" John said with a wink. "Stop biting your lip."

She nodded. "We'll still go over the mountain on the way home, won't we?"

"Yes, it should be a real nice drive."

"And you'll still take me to General Steam in the morning, too?"

He gave a tender smile. "Of course."

"Thanks."

"You going to be much longer?"

"No. I just need to think this through. Don't worry about the fire. You go to bed, and I'll cover it with dirt when I'm done."

After John left, Matthew sat beside her and said, "Julia, I'll be leaving in the morning, probably before you get up. I have a lot to do at the lab. Check with me tomorrow evening, and I'll probably have the verdict by then. With all the rain saturating the ground, there may not be anything left to report, you know."

"I know. I was worried about that," she said, nervously wiping her hands on her pants. "Actually, I was seriously considering giving up, but I know there's a story here. For some reason, someone is trying to stop me from doing any more research, and I'm not sure why. It's quite puzzling. The peculiar thing is that we've found nothing. We're at a standstill."

Matthew nodded, knowing their conversation had come to an end when she became quiet and looked into the fire pensively. He stood and headed for the back of his truck to get his sleeping bag.

As Julia watched the dying flames, she felt discouraged since they had found nothing. She knew that it probably would be wise to stop this search. Most people would, especially after receiving two threatening notes, being stalked, and having her car rammed. But not Julia. It sort of created a fire of curiosity inside her instead, and it would not leave.

Mr. Ponytail must have thought he was scaring her off, but it most definitely backfired. In fact, because of the notes and the ramming of her car, it sort of created a greater need to search out what it was that Mr. Ponytail was trying to hide. She never allowed fear to rule her or stop her from finding out the truth. She was a true reporter and curiosity overruled caution.

John, on the other hand, was a very cautious man. He

never liked danger or high places. He would have demanded Julia to stop this research if it would have done any good. Knowing her and her stubborn ways, he could not push her against her will. Personally, John never thought they were in any real danger, but now he was not so sure anymore. That's why they were heading home tomorrow.

Chapter 17

When the sun rose, it was another beautiful morning in the mountains. The birds were singing as if nothing was wrong with the world. John had risen before his wife and was making a warm fire; and Matthew had gone home. When Julia awoke, she sleepily headed for the river once again, but this time she searched the area thoroughly before she washed up. There was no sign of anyone, so she proceeded to clean herself up, washing the grime away from the day before. A breeze had blown off and on yesterday and whipped dust and dirt into her hair.

Julia grabbed her hairbrush and brushed through her tresses a few times, thinking perhaps it needed a shampoo. The last time she washed her hair in a mountain creek, it felt squeaky clean and softer than usual. As she remembered, the water had frozen her scalp, making her head tingle all over, but it sure felt refreshing afterward. How she hated dirty hair!

Without another thought, Julia leaned over the river and dunked her head in the running water. A sharp tingling sensation shot through her head and sent shivers up and down her spine several times. She squinted her eyes hard and moaned while the tingling sensation subsided. Why had she done such a thing?

"Oh, well, it's too late now," she groaned as she squirted biodegradable soap on her head and lathered up.

She quickly dunked her head in the river and let out another whimper. Then she wrung her hair and towel dried it. As she got to her feet, she heard a snort behind her. She gasped, dropping her towel to the ground. Julia jerked around and saw her husband walking toward her with a grin on his face, chuckling as he went.

When he got close enough, she slugged him on the shoulder and said in an exasperated tone, "You don't sneak up on a person like that, Mister!"

John had been watching her from a distance, trying to suppress his laughter the whole time as she groaned, moaned, and whimpered. That was when he snorted with humor. He probably shouldn't have been holding it in.

John chuckled and said, "You know what, Julia? I don't understand how you women can wash in freezing-cold water. It's too dad-blame cold for me to try something like that."

Then he shivered, just thinking about it, and shook his head in wonderment.

Julia smiled at his reaction. "It's not that bad, John. Afterwards, you feel tingly and refreshed. Besides, the torture is minimal and well worth it. Actually, it feels so good to be clean again." Then she stuck her chin in the air, smiled, and gave John a smug look. "I guess it's something a man could never endure. Pain, that is! When it comes to pain, women are the warriors." Then she snickered.

John grinned, noticing how her eyes had brightened and her cheeks were rosy from the cold water. She was playing with him, teasing him. She seemed to be in a good mood this morning, much better than last night. Her attitude seemed to be improving. Searching her eyes, he could see the sparkle of mischief in them, and that made him smile.

"All right, Julia, if you think you can smile at me like that and get away with it, you're dreadfully mistaken."

Then he playfully grabbed her shoulders, pulled her close, and kissed her soundly on the lips. As he held her, he could feel the tension in her shoulders and that worried him. Trying to get a good story was not worth all this stress, but how was he going to tell her without her independence kicking in? He leaned back and looked into her eyes.

"You're a little tense, Julia."

"I know," she said as she rubbed the muscles in her neck. "I didn't sleep well last night. The ground felt harder than usual."

What an excuse! He pulled her close and gently massaged her neck, shoulders, and back, trying to release the stiff muscles. He could feel a knot between her shoulders, and he tried to work it out.

As John massaged, she winced a few times. These were muscles that had stiffened during the past few days. The pressures of this assignment, trying to get a good story, and sitting at her desk longer than usual had taken their toll on Julia. As her muscles began to loosen, the pain gradually subsided, and she sighed with relief.

John leaned back and asked with concern, "Do you feel better?"

"Uh-huh. Much."

"Good. I hate to see you this way, Julia. This assignment is putting too much pressure on you."

"Don't worry so much. I'm all right. Really, I am," she replied, trying to sound confident.

When John frowned and shook his head, she could see doubt written all over his face. So just to convince him and prove that she was feeling better, she placed her hands on both sides of his cheeks and kissed him, giving a lingering and satisfying kiss.

As John wrapped his arms around her, he gave in to the delicious warmth spreading through him. If she were trying to prove that she was feeling all right, she was succeeding.

John leaned back and looked into her eyes as he said his famous statement, "I'll give you an hour to stop that."

She smiled at his sense of humor.

When John looked into her eyes, he gave her the message of adoring love as he studied every contour of her face.

"I'm sure glad you're feeling better, Sweetheart." His eyes trailed down to her mouth as he said, "You're not joshing me, are you?"

"No, why would I...?"

Julia's words were muffled when she felt his mouth touch hers. She gradually melted in his arms as he embraced her and gave her a tender but passionate kiss, making her feel loved and protected. As he gently caressed her back, she responded and slid her fingers through his thick wavy hair. He instantly tightened his arms around her, pulling her close to his chest.

John knew that love and tenderness went a long way with a woman. The love he felt for his wife was insurmountable. Their marriage was like any other; they had to work at it, learn to give and take, forgive one another, and overlook one another's faults and failings. To look for the good in one another was an everlasting goal for them, not to mention trying to support one another's dreams. To John, she was his equal, but deep inside, he looked up to her as a stronger and more spiritual person than he.

As John held her lovingly in his arms, it seemed as if no one in the world existed but the two of them. As a rush of love spread through him, he gave in to the delightful sensation he was feeling … and then Julia's cell phone rang, interrupting them with an annoying ring.

He very seldom had private time with her because of his late hours at work, and this precious time together while camping was now being interrupted by a blasted phone call. All he wanted to do was grab that annoying phone and toss it in the river. Then he would pick her up and carry her to the tent and kiss all that tension away.

When John leaned back and looked into her eyes, he grinned. He saw how his kiss and tender caresses had affected her, and he was happy they still had that same old romance in their lives after all these years.

He lightly touched his fingers to the velvety curves of her face as he whispered, "Ignore it, Sweetheart."

Julia gave an apologetic smile and said breathlessly, "Excuse me, Romeo, but I really have to answer this."

"Excuse me!" John said teasingly as he entangled his fingers in her wet auburn hair. "But I'd rather be compared to Crocodile Dundee or Indiana Jones if you don't mind. Romeo's a sissy."

Julia grinned. "Okay, Dundee."

He chuckled. "Now that's better."

"I think April's probably worried and just checking up on us."

"Let her worry. It's good for her." John pulled her closer and whispered, "Now I'd like to take care of some unfinished business if you don't mind. Where did we leave off?"

With that, he started nibbling at her ear, sending a chill up her spine.

Julia shook her head and pushed him back. "I can't do that to April. She knows that I've been threatened, and I can't let her worry."

As John reluctantly released his hold on her, he licked his lips, savoring the taste of his wife's kiss.

Then he sighed, "I understand."

Julia grabbed her wet towel and then answered the phone as she slid her hand in John's and walked back to camp.

He squeezed her hand lovingly, wishing he could continue their little romantic interlude, but knowing Julia, it would be pointless. She already had her mind on other things at the moment, and he knew there would be no persuading her to his way of thinking. Not now, anyway. Blast it all! Too bad she had the stupid phone with her.

After she hung up, John smiled. "I fixed breakfast while you were torturing yourself at the river."

She laughed. "Sounds great."

"How are the kids?"

"Good!"

"April?"

"Worried."

"Well, after we eat, I'll take you to see the old mining community."

"Sounds good to me."

John turned toward her with astonishment as her cell phone let out three beeps and died. He chuckled. It finally died! Good! A little too late, though! But better late than never! Since they were taking the long way home over the mountain, he planned on finding a secluded spot, and they would have a little romantic time together.

After a delicious meal of orange juice, sausages, and eggs, John took down the tent while Julia packed the sleeping bags and food. As she put everything in the back of the truck, she wondered about the yellow Hummer. Would they run into it on the way over the mountain?

She was feeling a little discouraged because she had found nothing in the way of pollution or animal carcasses. Julia shook her head in despair. She thought for sure they would have found something up and down the creek, but they hadn't. She knew that Bill would have her discontinue the search and call it an accidental spilling. In fact, Julia was mostly worried what Ted would say when she got back. She could just hear him say, "I told you so."

Julia cringed at the thought of it. She was always bested by that ridiculous man; bested by everything he said and did. Why couldn't she have her turn with a great story once in a while?

As she set the backpacks in the back of the truck, John saw her discouraged face. "What's wrong, Julia? And don't say it's nothing. I know you better than that."

She gave a slight smile. "You can always tell when I'm discouraged."

John dumped the tent in the back of the truck and then took her hand in his and led her to a folding chair. He sat down and pulled her onto his lap. "Tell me about it."

Julia laughed. "We're going to break this chair. I don't think it can hold the two of us."

"I don't care. I want to know what's bothering you, and I won't let you go until you tell me. Is it this assignment?"

"Really, it's nothing. It's no big deal."

John shook his head stubbornly. "I don't believe you."

When they both heard a creak from the folding chair, she warned, "John, it isn't going to hold us."

He grinned smugly as he heard another low creak from the chair.

"I really don't want to talk about it."

John held tightly around her waist and shimmied back and forth, making the chair squeak and groan.

Julia's eyes widened when she saw his teasing grin. "All right, you win. Stop jiggling the chair."

He stopped. "Okay. I'm listening."

Julia relaxed into his arms and said softly, "I have nothing for my article. Matthew and I searched diligently, and we found nothing. He even suggested that any evidence that might have been here is now gone, that it might be a wild goose chase. He didn't seem very positive about it last night. And personally, I don't feel very positive either."

"So what's bothering you? That you may not have a story, or having to tell Ted that it was all for nothing?"

Julia hesitated. She didn't want to admit it, but he hit it right on the nose. She reluctantly nodded, lowering her eyes in shame. "Both, but it's also more than that."

"I'm still listening, Julia."

"Why did that man in the Mercedes want me to stop searching? Why was I threatened? I have no proof of anything. The only reason I decided to go further was because of the old man's report and the two threatening notes, not to mention being rammed on the road.

Something deep inside me wants to continue."

"Don't worry about the man in the Mercedes. The police will take care of it. After I reported it, they said they would do what they could and be on the lookout. But without a license plate number, they didn't have much to go on."

"I know. I was too frazzled and upset to notice the license plate. Besides, he was following too close."

John nodded and said, "I don't think this trip was all for nothing. I've had a grand old time. I found myself a cave and a bunch of money."

When she saw him grinning from ear to ear, she punched him on the shoulder and smiled.

John chuckled. "I knew I could get a smile out of you yet."

As they both laughed, the chair creaked even louder and before either one could blink an eye, the chair collapsed under them. John fell backwards. Julia was stunned, but after getting over the initial surprise, they burst into laughter.

"I told you this chair wouldn't hold the two of us."

"You see how much fun we've had?" John laughed as he gave her a quick kiss on the nose.

They both clumsily arose from the flattened chair, and he tossed it in the back of the truck. After loading everything, Julia walked to the passenger side and opened the door.

As John climbed in, he said, "I thought we could do a little target shooting at General Steam."

"That sounds fun."

He grabbed his revolver under the seat and clipped the holster to his belt. "Remember all that shaving cream I brought? We'll have a blast."

"Why shaving cream?"

"Oh, Julia, you'll love it. When you hit it, the cream spurts out and white foam sprays everywhere. It's awesome!"

She laughed at his enthusiasm.

As they drove down the road, he told her that it wasn't too far from their campsite. After finding a convenient place to park on the side of the road, Julia hung the camera strap over her shoulder and her canteen over her neck while John grabbed a bag of shaving cream and soda cans.

They crossed the road and stood beside an old juniper tree, looking across a small gully to the other side where large pieces of rusted iron parts were strewn along the desert ground from years past. A few wooden buildings stood here and there on the side of the mountain in bad repair. Since the community was so small, it was easy to see the whole layout from there.

As John pointed out the mining community to Julia, something did not feel right to him. What it was, he was not sure. He sensed it more than anything. They were about to climb down the small slope and cross the river when John grabbed her arm and pulled her behind a juniper.

Julia looked up at him curiously, and he put his finger to his lips and hushed her quietly. He pulled her toward a few thick shrubs and stooped down. She did likewise. He laid his bag of soda cans on the ground and then spread the bushes apart slightly. He carefully studied the area, looking at every inch of the layout. Then his eyes widened.

Chapter 18

John tensed as he surveyed the area and saw what he was searching for. He leaned toward his wife and whispered, "This place is supposed to be deserted and it isn't. You see all those vehicles at the side of the main building? And there's the yellow Hummer, too. Maybe old man Jones isn't so crazy after all."

"What do you mean?" Julia whispered.

"The police didn't give him the time of day, so I didn't give it much credibility either. I guess I should have listened."

She quickly scanned the mining community and asked, "What's that pond?"

John studied it for a while. "Hmmm. It could be a leach pond. I've seen one at USMX."

"USMX?"

"It's the name of a mining company not far from here. They were mining gold. It's been shut down for some time, though."

"A leach pond?" Julia said thoughtfully as she stared at it.

"It leaches gold out of ore and…" He looked at her as if stunned.

"What is it, John?"

"Well, what do ya know!"

"What, what?" she asked anxiously.

"Julia, a leach pond leaches gold out of ore, and what's left inside the pond is cyanide."

"Cyanide?"

"Yup. Cyanide!" He thought for a moment and then asked, "Did you say all this cyanide poisoning happened just before the flood?"

"Yes."

"Okay. That's it! This is how I see it. We had a long spell of constant rain before the flooding. It rained so much that it filled these leach ponds. It overflowed from the heavy rain and got into the river system. It killed a few fish and some animals, and the long rain spell we had swooshed everything away, leaving no evidence of the poisoning. The whole thing was an accidental spilling caused by too much rain."

"An accident?" Julia said with disappointment.

"That's what I think." When he saw the forlorn look on her face, he said, "Sorry to crush your bubble."

"Crush?" she asked mournfully.

He nodded.

"Then if that's the case, why don't these men want me finding out about their little operation? Mining gold isn't against the law, so why threaten me?"

"You've got a point there."

Julia thought for a moment and then her eyes brightened and she smiled.

John knew that look of triumph. "What is it?"

"I've got it. In my book, I had the bad guys pretend to have a legal operation going on to hide the illegal operation."

John grinned at her imagination. "So, you believe they're hiding something illegal behind this façade?"

"That's right. Perhaps they're afraid that I might get too close. I might find out something that an ordinary person would overlook. I'm a reporter and they know I'm looking for a story."

John's shoulders bounced with breathless laughter without making a sound. "I know. How can I forget?" Then he got to his feet and whispered, "You stay here. I'll go check it out."

"What?" she said with disbelief. "You're not leaving me here, John. I want to be part of this."

He shook his head. "What if you happen to be right … which I personally think you aren't. I don't want any harm to come to you. If they're as desperate as you say, then we'll both be in trouble. It'll be up to you to get help."

Julia knew he was right, so she conceded. "But don't get too close. Okay?"

John nodded and walked silently down the slope. Julia snapped a few pictures of the other side of the gully. Scattered among this dry desert land, she saw gears lying about and a rusted steam generator with iron wheels. In days gone by, it was used to generate electricity to run the machinery.

As she zoomed her camera in closer, she could see that one cylinder was open at both ends, with a firebrick lining. It was large enough for her to walk inside without bending over. Amazing!

* * *

John knew every inch of General Steam. It was a small,

abandoned community, and he had come here several times with Paul. Only a half dozen buildings were still standing since most had rotted and fallen to the ground.

He carefully crossed the creek, working his way through the desert brush and growth until he saw a bunch of bushes at the top of the gully.

When he finally stopped at a creosote bush, he separated the limbs and peered through the opening. He remained in this spot for quite a while and watched what was going on. There was very little activity, just a few men stirring about and others sleeping lazily in the midday sun. Everything looked harmless. As he watched, he felt confused. What was he supposed to be looking for in the first place?

The dampness clung to his skin as the sun bore down on his back. He pulled his handkerchief from his pocket and wiped the beads of sweat from his brow. He stuffed the handkerchief back and was about to leave when he felt a tap on his shoulder that made him jump and suck in his breath.

"John," came the whisper.

He turned around with an exasperated look and whispered breathlessly, "Julia! You scared the bee-gee-bees out of me. I thought you were going to stay put."

"I was until I saw something peculiar. I thought I should let you know." She handed him the binoculars and said, "I got these from the truck. Look at that cabin over there." She pointed to a small structure a ways off. "I saw a man walk out and then bolt the door shut before leaving. There's a two by four placed into a couple slots."

"That's odd."

"Not only that, he was wearing a holster on his hip." Julia

pointed towards the building.

John put the binoculars to his eyes and was able to spy the building she had pointed out. Sure enough, it was bolted shut.

He looked at Julia questioningly.

"I think there's someone inside," she said. "Otherwise, why bolt it?"

John rubbed his chin in thought, wondering if his wife's imagination was getting away with her. "And you think we should check it out?"

She nodded.

"Is anyone standing guard or close by?"

"No." She pointed to a large storage building. "The man went inside that building over there. Everything's clear by the cabin."

The large storage building she had pointed to was once used as a main office for the mining company. John looked through the binoculars once again, slowly scanning the whole area. She was right. He turned to her and saw the hopeful look in her eyes.

John smiled and nodded. "Okay, I'll take a look. I'll be right back."

As he started toward the building, he heard Julia close behind him. He turned around and whispered, "Julia, you have to stay here."

"What if you need help?"

"I won't. If something happens, then take the truck and go after help. Got it?"

Julia nodded and slunk back behind the bushes and watched.

John looked around and saw no one in sight, so he quickly tiptoed around to the back of the small cabin. It was an old, dilapidated building with a partially boarded-up window. It had small spaces between the wallboards, most of them rotting. He pressed his face against one of the cracks and peered through the wall. Light was shining through and he was able to make out certain shapes.

He slowly scanned the inside of the small, darkened building. When he came upon a lump on the floor, he turned white and gasped. A sinking feeling overtook him, and he felt empty inside. Without hesitation, he began pulling at the rotten boards one at a time and placed them on the ground. Each board came loose with very little effort. After pulling off several boards, he was able to squeeze through the gaping hole.

Chapter 19

John silently and carefully crawled to the lump on the ground. He untied the man's ankles and wrists and pulled the gag from his mouth. Then he whispered, "What are you doing here?"

The man rubbed his wrists and ankles to quickly bring the circulation back and then whispered. "Well, as I was driving home, I came upon a four-wheeler that was sitting in the middle of the road. They said they had engine troubles so I tried to help and this is where I ended up."

"I don't understand."

"Well," Matthew shook his head in despair. "They said I shouldn't have been snooping around with that woman reporter. The leader looked like he wanted to get rid of me, but the others stopped him, saying their boss wouldn't like it. I struggled and tried to get loose, but they crowned me one. The next thing I knew, I woke up in here."

John's eyes widened at what he had just heard. This was not what he had expected when he said he would check things out for his wife. Whatever was going on wasn't good.

"How did you know I was here?" asked Matthew.

"Julia saw a man leave and bolt the door behind him."

"Oh, yeah. He was questioning me, trying to find out what

I knew and what Julia had found out." He touched a red bruise on his cheek. "I told him that we knew nothing, but he didn't believe me. He thought he could beat it out of me but finally gave up."

"What oafs!" He helped Matthew to his feet as he said, "Let's get outta here."

"I'm with you," he whispered. "But first, we have to find out what's going on. Why have they threatened Julia … and now me?"

"No!" John shook his head adamantly. "We're not staying and finding out anything, Matt."

Matthew shook his head with disapproval. "If you don't find out what's going on, then Julia may never be safe."

John hesitated for a few seconds and then peeked through the slats and said, "You're right. Have you been watching them through these cracks?"

"Yes. Right now, they're lying around resting, but most of the activity seems to be around that large building. They've been taking boxes of stuff and loading it into the back of a truck. I heard someone say their cover was up and they had to get out fast!"

John leaned closer to the open crack and nodded. "I see the truck. Do you have any idea what they're loading?"

"Not sure, but I heard one of the head honchos yelling at a guy, saying to be careful because they were priceless. He was real upset."

"Priceless?"

His brow creased as his mind turned to Paul. *You could call them pirates. Thugs! Looters! Louts! It's illegal to collect artifacts, whether on government land or private.*

John looked through the crack once again and then

turned to Matthew. "Could it be artifacts by any chance?"

Matthew shrugged. "Don't know for sure. That's all I heard. When someone mentioned how priceless this shipment was, he said they could be rich after this load, so I just figured they were mining gold." He thought for a moment and his eyes brightened. "As I think about it, I saw one man carrying a couple of pots inside the main building. He was told to pack it with Styrofoam."

"Pots?" John's eyes were wide with concern. "If these are the same men who have been digging at the site, they must be hiding the artifacts here and using this area as a cover for mining. That would be the reason why they didn't want Julia to do any snooping." He shook his head in despair. "How ironic!"

"What?"

John sighed with exasperation. "This was exactly what I've been trying to protect Julia from this whole time, and here we are right in the middle of it." He groaned and then looked at Matthew and said with a warning voice, "Matthew, if I'm correct, these men are dangerous."

"What should we do?"

"Well, the only phone we have just died right after Julia spoke to April this morning. Do you have yours?"

Matthew shook his head. "They took it from me."

John pursed his lips in thought. "First off, you and Julia are going back to the truck to get help. I'll stay and watch at a safe distance so I can report anything I find. Go directly to Paul. He's got an investigator whose pursuing this. He'll be in charge and will get the help we need. Got it?"

"Yes."

John patted Matthew's back with encouragement and then

both men slipped out of the hole and scurried toward the bushes where Julia was hidden. When they approached, she was wide-eyed with wonder when they plopped to their knees beside her.

"Matthew? What are you doing here?" she said incredulously.

"He was captured by those louts," said John as he waved a hand toward the main building.

"Captured?" asked Julia. "By whom?"

"Artifact pirates. Looters."

Julia's heart picked up speed as she said, "What's going on here, John."

"Well, you were right. It looks like they used this place as a cover. But something went wrong. You got in the way. Matthew's been watching, and he says it looks like they're going to move out, artifacts and all. We can't let them do that. I want you and Matthew to get help."

"What? I can't leave you here alone," she said with concern.

Seeing the worry in his wife's eyes, he took her by the shoulders, kissed her lips, and said, "I'll be fine. Don't worry about me."

"I don't feel good about leaving you here, John."

He smiled and touched her cheek affectionately. "I'll be careful. Now get going. Tell Paul to hurry."

Julia nodded. She knew he was right, but she would be back with Paul and the authorities. This was a story of a lifetime and nothing would keep her away. How about her husband, though? Would he be safe while they were getting help? Worry began eating at her as she reluctantly followed Matthew. *Please let him be safe*, she whispered.

John settled down behind a thick shrub and watched the main building. After ten minutes, he heard rustling of leaves behind him, and he turned to find his wife heading toward him.

He frowned as he asked, "What's going on? Where's Matthew?"

Julia shrugged. "We got separated."

"Separated? How?"

Julia bit her lip nervously. "Please don't be upset with me, but I couldn't leave you behind. What if something happened to you? I would never forgive myself." She glanced at the ground and said softly, "So I told Matthew to go without me."

When John saw the worry and anxiety in her eyes, he realized that he couldn't be upset. Yes, she was stubborn, all right. But he could see how concerned she was by leaving him. He smiled and patted the ground beside him.

After she settled down, he pointed in the direction of the storage building. "There must be another door on the side of that building because I don't see anyone coming and going. I'm going over there and check it out. If you would, I'd appreciate it if you could stay put behind these bushes and look out for me at this end. You're well hidden here, and it might be safer than with me. If you see anyone coming in my direction, whistle. Not a long one, but a short quick one, just so they don't know where it came from. Okay?"

She nodded.

"Can you whistle?"

She puckered and gave a short low whistle. It wasn't much, but it was whistle.

John smiled as he took her hand and squeezed it. "That'll

do. Now don't move from this spot. Got it?"

She bit her lip nervously. "Got it."

John smiled and whispered, "Stop biting your lip, Julia. Everything's going to be okay. I'll be careful."

When he turned to leave, she tugged on his shirtsleeve, and he turned to face her. Then she whispered, "I love you. Please don't take any chances."

John smiled one of his crooked smiles. "I won't."

Then he took off toward the storage building without a sound. Julia watched him until he walked to the other side of the building and was out of sight. She knew approximately where he was, so if anyone went that direction, she would warn him. She took a drink from her canteen that hung around her neck and then knelt on her knees and peered through the bushes. She took a few pictures of the site and anything suspicious. The place was peaceful and quiet. After five minutes had gone by, she set her camera down and sat back on her haunches, watching for any sign of movement.

As Julia sat quietly watching the area, she felt a sharp jab against her back. Thinking it was Matthew and that he had returned for some reason, she slowly turned around and her eyes widened. She gasped, instantly putting her hand to her mouth.

The burly man behind her was holding a rifle in his hand and grinning, showing his yellow teeth. She had seen this man before. He was large, powerful, and unshaven. This man looked like a hard case as he spat black tobacco juice out of the corner of his mouth, which landed only inches from her knees. His dark, hollow eyes were hard with no compassion, and his unrelenting expression was frightening. It did not take long for her to realize that he was the same man at the parking lot.

"Well, well. What do we have here?" Johnson growled, with sarcasm lacing his voice. He pushed the tobacco into the side of his cheek and then demanded, "Git on your feet, lady! When I show the boss who I've got, he'll be pleased."

Julia's heart was pounding, as it had never done before. She felt anxiety rising within her, and the feeling of terror that rose in her chest made it hard to breathe. There seemed to be a dark cloud hovering over her, and she could do nothing about it. At that moment, she felt her future was very bleak. This man was powerful, and there was no way she could get away. What was she to do?

"Git on your feet, lady," he repeated irritably.

As Julia cautiously stood, she tried to control her trembling hands, but it was useless. As her heart twisted, she realized that she had to be brave and not give in to her fears. To show fear showed weakness and to show weakness made one vulnerable to the evil of these men. She had to fight the increasing panic that rose inside her. She needed to get a hold of herself. She took a deep breath and then stuck her chin in the air to show that she was not frightened.

The man chuckled at her attitude and motioned toward the main building. "We're taking a little jaunt, Mrs. Evans."

Julia's eyes widened as her mind worked feverishly for a way out of this predicament. Instantly, an idea came to her mind. The adrenaline caused by her stress was rushing through her veins, giving her enough energy to do what she had planned.

Julia looked over the burly man's shoulder with hope in her eyes and a smile, as if someone were standing in back of him. It worked perfectly. When he saw her look, he immediately looked over his shoulder to see who was there.

When he turned his head, Julia quickly pushed the rifle aside with her left hand. At the same instant, she lunged forward with all the energy and strength she could muster and swung her right foot upwards into his groin, forcing him to double over. The burly man groaned as he fell to his knees, writhing and moaning in pain. With his head bent toward the ground, he began cursing a string of expletives that burned Julia's ears. She winced from the vile words that spewed from his mouth and instantly pulled her canteen off her neck and pounded the cursing man's head a few times.

When he dropped to the ground, smashing his face into the dirt, she tossed her canteen to the ground. Then she quickly twisted her body around and took off with great speed, only to land into the solid chest of a well-built man with a broad grin on his face. He was unusually tall, dressed in white pants with a ponytail hanging down his back.

He grabbed her by the arms and began laughing in a most hearty manner, as if he were amused by her actions.

Chapter 20

"This one's got spunk," Devollyn said admiringly, as he firmly held Julia by the upper arms.

The man on the ground groaned as he got to his feet, wiping the dust from his face and clothes and cursing with vehemence. He rubbed the sore spot on the back of his head and said gruffly, "Boss, let me at her."

"No," Devollyn said firmly. "You're not touching this one."

"Why? Did you see what she did to me?"

"Yes, I did," he said firmly. "She almost got away, too. It seems you can't do a job right."

The burly man stared at Julia with a fierce look in his eyes, his fists clenching and unclenching angrily. His penetrating glare unnerved her, and his loud breathing was labored, as if he was ready to pounce on her. Julia knew that if his boss wasn't there, she wouldn't see tomorrow.

It did not last long because Devollyn growled, "No one, and I mean no one, is touching this lady. Do you understand?"

Johnson gave a curt nod but was not happy about it. He turned and limped away as he rubbed the back of his sore head.

When Julia turned to the tall man standing beside her, he looked as if he were quite amused at the situation.

"You certainly know how to defend yourself, don't you, Mrs. Evans?" Devollyn said with a bit of humor in his voice.

With defiance, Julia said, "I try."

"Remember me?"

"You're the man who tried to run me off the road in the white Mercedes," she said accusingly.

"Correction. I was only trying to scare you. That's all. Nothing more. I wouldn't have hurt you, Mrs. Evans."

"I don't believe you."

"I was hoping you would abandon your research, but like a true reporter, you didn't. I should have figured that. The fact is, I have a big order to take care of and I couldn't have any complications."

"And I was that complication?" she asked heatedly.

"Yes, Ma'am. You were."

He took her firmly by the upper arm and led her toward the main building located at the center of the mining community.

Julia glared at Mr. Ponytail and asked in a firm, unwavering voice, "Since I'm a complication, what are you going to do with me?"

"I'm still thinking on that one. I haven't made up my mind as of yet. Depends."

"Depends on what?"

"My mood and how fast we can get out of here. We've done all we can, so we're packing up and taking off in the morning. Until then, we'll tie you up until I make up my mind what to do with you." Devollyn stopped and turned to Julia. "Mrs. Evans, I really don't want to hurt you."

"Why are you giving me a chance? I know too much. Why not kill me now?"

Devollyn chuckled at her spunk. "If I'm caught for artifact theft, I'll be fined. But murder would land me in jail without much of a chance to get out. That's not my style."

He nudged her onward, holding tight to her upper arm. After a moment of silence, he looked at Julia suspiciously.

"By the way, where's your husband, if I may ask?"

"He went for help," she lied.

"Oh? And left you to watch after me? I doubt that very much."

"We let Matthew go and he's gone after help, too."

"Are you sure about that?" Devollyn grinned. "I've got men at the entrance of the canyon watching for your husband. He hasn't a chance of escape. And besides that, I'm sure he wouldn't leave you alone here by yourself. It's not safe, as you well know."

Devollyn opened the door to the large spacious building and nudged her inside. As Julia entered, she gasped. Matthew was tied to a chair. Help was not on the way, after all. Julia's heart sank as she realized what a mess she had gotten herself into.

When Devollyn saw her forlorn look, he chuckled. "Hey, cheer up. It's not all that bad. It could be worse."

"How could it be worse? A notorious thief has the upper hand. It couldn't get much worse if you ask me."

His smile widened as he said, "Come with me. I've got something to show you."

He took her by the arm and led her into a small room that had been used as an office many years ago. In the corner were a variety of antiquities. The room was swept clean, and there was a makeshift table and a camping chair beside it. In the corner was a cot with a pillow and a blanket. A suitcase was opened and inside were clothes neatly folded in piles.

As her eyes scanned the room, she said sarcastically, "I can say one thing for you. You're neat and clean … that is, for a crook."

"No, a collector, my dear. There's a difference," he corrected with emphasis. "Do you want to see my treasures? The ones that are being packed will be sold to my clients in Las Vegas, Chicago, and Phoenix, but this stash is mine. I won't part with these beauties. They're perfect in every way, not a crack or chip on them. Let me show you."

He led her to the corner and waved his hand in front of his treasures. There were colorful pots of every size, baskets made of yucca fiber, and delicate pendants.

"Aren't they beautiful?" Devollyn asked, his eyes glowing with pride. He led her to an ancient skull and carefully picked it up with both hands. "Isn't it something?"

After letting her look at it for a minute, he carefully placed it back on the floor with the other artifacts.

When he saw Julia staring at one of the necklaces, he handed it to her. "This pendant was sealed in a pottery jar. It was buried beneath the remains of a small pueblo. We were lucky to find it."

The necklace had red and black bead-like stones threaded on a string made of yucca plant. Suspended from the string was a red pendant made from a pottery shard and carved perfectly in a triangle shape

Julia looked at the intricate work and an overwhelming feeling touched her heart. Then it dawned on her. This was the same pendant that she had dreamed about. There was something special about this necklace. She just knew it. But what was it? The warm sensation she felt was like no other, a sacred feeling, an impression ... sort of like a message from the dust.

Why had she dreamed about this necklace? Was it for a reason? What did it represent to the woman who wore it? There was an answer to her question. There had to be.

"Well? What do you think of it?"

"They were talented people." She looked up and said accusingly, "And you're stealing it, taking away valuable history for the public to see."

Devollyn's eyes darkened, as if annoyed by her attitude. "The museums have plenty." He took the pendant from her hand and carefully placed it along with the others. "I'm a collector. I've collected many fine treasures."

"You're a thief and nothing more."

Devollyn scowled. "I'm not the bad guy, Mrs. Evans."

"Then if you're not the bad guy, who are you?"

"I'm a businessman. I have clients who pay big bucks for what I dig up. As long as I have customers to keep me in business, why should I quit?"

"How did you get into this business in the first place?"

"I've always been a lover of antiquities. I have workers under me and I have buyers. It's as simple as that."

Julia shook her head in disgust. "You keep referring to yourself as a collector. What you're doing is stealing and against the law."

Devollyn cursed, losing his tempter at her ignorance. "That law is outdated. It was made over a hundred years ago."

Feeling impatient, he grabbed her arm and pushed her

toward the door. "I'm not the only one who thinks the law should be revised. If people didn't want it so badly, I wouldn't have a job." He stopped at the doorway and waved his hand toward a bunch of boxes at the corner of the room. "Treasures like these should be open for the public to buy."

"And when it's all gone, then what?"

"I wouldn't worry about it. As I said, the museums have plenty."

After grabbing a chair and some twine, Devollyn tugged her along. Julia felt like a rag doll being led about. Out of frustration, she pulled herself from his grasp, but he quickly grabbed hold of her arm and squeezed. The pressure of his hand caused her to grimace.

As he led her toward Matthew, Julia thought about the relics and tried to think of a way to save them. She quickly scanned the room. There had to be a way out. Devollyn could not get away with this. She had to stop him, but how?

As he dropped the chair in place, he motioned to it and said, "We can do this the easy way or the hard way. It's up to you, Mrs. Evans."

Julia reluctantly sat down. Then he pulled a switchblade from his pocket, popped it open, and cut a piece of twine. He knelt down beside her and firmly tied her wrists.

Devollyn looked up at her and shook his head with wonder as he said, "I've never met a she-cat like you before. I believe you maimed Johnson in more ways than one. You injured his ego, and I think he'll try to get even."

Julia was sick and tired of being threatened and fearing for her life. She narrowed her eyes and said, "I know you were watching our camp."

Devollyn smiled. "That was Johnson. As he passed your truck, he saw you. I told him to scare you away, not to harm you. We weren't done here and I needed more time. So Johnson's been trying a variety of things to frighten you off, such as putting a rattlesnake by your tent, but apparently it didn't work." He shook his head in regret. "While you're here, I'll do my best to protect you. I wouldn't make Johnson angry again. He doesn't respect women like I do, so I'd watch my tongue if I were you."

Julia laughed mockingly and said, "Respect? You don't even know what the word means. You don't have respect for ancient history."

"Of course I do," he growled. "I have great respect for it. This is how I earn my living."

Julia closed her eyes and didn't want to look at the man any longer. She was sick of his lawless attitude and his superior manners. She was now his prisoner, and she could do nothing to protect the artifacts. It was now up to John, wherever he was.

The oppressive feeling that overtook Julia made her feel helpless. She could not allow this feeling to press her down into a state of depression. There just had to be a way out.

"There's no escape," Devollyn commented matter-of-factly as he tied her ankles together. "If perchance you could get loose, the area is heavily guarded. I wouldn't attempt it if I were you. My men would shoot you down without question. When I'm not around, they do as they please."

After she was tied securely, he stood and smiled. "That should hold you, I believe."

Then he turned around and meandered off, waking his men and giving orders to begin loading the truck with artifacts.

Julia looked over at Matthew and said softly, "I'm so sorry I got you into this."

Matthew was gagged, but he nodded as if he understood. She looked around for some way out, feeling frustrated, wondering where her husband was and if he was all right. How did she get herself into this predicament in the first place? Curiosity and wanting a good story was her answer.

As she looked around the building, Julia tried to think of a way to save the artifacts. These thieves could not get away with this, but how could she stop them? She struggled to get her hands free, twisting and pulling, but the twine only cut into her wrists and a sharp pain shot through her hands. It was hopeless.

Julia thought about her plight. She felt no fear toward Devollyn, but his henchmen were a completely different story. The way Johnson looked at her gave her the creeps. She knew that money ruled their lives, and she feared those men most of all.

Chapter 21

The anger and fury John felt was beyond words. They had taken his most prized possession, the love of his life. He berated himself for being so foolish as to let her stay behind while he checked out the goings-on. He should have taken her with him. He nervously paced back and forth, wondering what to do.

John knew she had been taken against her will because she had left her camera next to the shrub, slightly hidden from sight. She would never have left that behind. And besides that, the canteen was grossly dented in, and the ground showed there had been a scuffle of some sort right where he had left her.

When John had sneaked over to the main building to see what was going on, he found about half a dozen men lying around and resting; some were sound asleep. After a few minutes, the leader of the bunch awakened them and told them to get busy loading the truck again. John was only gone for half an hour, and when he came back, Julia was gone. He was sick with worry, blaming himself for not taking her along.

The only thing he could do was to search for her. So he ducked down and crept from one desert plant to another, stopping and listening carefully at each bush before continuing on. When he felt safe, he continued on to the next juniper until he came upon the large dilapidated structure. He silently crept down the slope toward the center building and peeked through a knothole. He could see nothing where he was, so he moved farther south and peeked through a crack in the wall. There she was, neatly tied up and sitting on a chair, looking so helpless that it made his heart wrench inside. Then, when he saw Matthew, his heart sank. Help was not on the way after all. What was he to do?

John knew he had to get them out of there, but how? All the men were now awake. There was a back door to the building, but there was no way he could sneak in without being detected. As he peered through the crack, trying to think of a plan, he saw a tall man in white walk into the building and speak to the men.

"I see that you're almost done here," said Devollyn. "I've sent a bunch of men to search the canyon for Mr. Evans. I know that he won't go far since his wife is here, so it shouldn't be difficult to find him. I've got them searching the mouth of the canyon. Besides, he couldn't go far even if he wanted to, since we put his vehicle out of commission."

Then he waved his hand toward the door and said, "You three load the truck. The others have done a sloppy job and I want you to reorganize the boxes and push them closer together toward the front of the cab so we can fit in more boxes. We need to make room for some of the men to fit back there when we take off tomorrow morning. Right now, I'm going to town and grabbing a bite to eat. I'll bring back food for the rest of you before dark." He turned toward Johnson, pointed to him, and said, "You're in charge while I'm gone."

Devollyn turned on his heels and strode outside; each step was long and with purpose. The men watched him leave, feeling his air of authority.

Then Johnson turned to his men and said, "Follow me. I want you to organize the truck while I finish packing the artifacts in boxes."

John watched the men leave as he peered through the crack, trying to think of a way to distract them and get Julia and Matthew out of there. As he heard the burly man giving orders, he began to conjure up a plan. He had to make sure he carefully planned out everything. If anything went wrong, it could mean the lives of everyone.

***

Johnson explained to the men that they needed to rearrange a few of the boxes before they could put new ones in. He pointed to a bunch sitting on the ground beside the truck, which needed to be packed. After much deliberation, he strode toward the building and walked through the door. He stopped long enough to sneer at Julia. His eyes were hard and cold as he glared at her. And then he turned toward the tall pile of boxes filled with artifacts.

Julia cleared her throat and said softly, "I'm sorry that I hurt you."

That took Johnson aback, and he turned toward her in surprise.

She swallowed and tried again, "Really. I didn't mean to hurt you. I did it out of self-preservation."

"Self what?" he growled.

"Self-preservation. I didn't want to be your prisoner, so I

fought back. Wouldn't you if you were in my situation?"

Johnson grunted. "Don't try to get on my good side, lady. It won't work. Besides, you're safe enough as long as thick-headed Devollyn has a say in it. Personally, I would have done away with you long ago."

"You see? That's just what I meant. I did it out of self-preservation."

He grinned with amusement, understanding what she was saying. "He's a fool, I tell ya."

"Who is?"

"Devollyn. That's why you're still alive. But he's a bare-faced fool, if you ask me." He scowled and added, "You could mess up everything for us, and he doesn't see that. He's too afraid of having murder attached to his name. Why didn't you take the hint, lady? Threatening notes! Ramming your car! I even let you know I was stalking you, but you didn't give up. Why?"

Julia shrugged. "I'm a reporter. What can I say?"

With an irritated tone, he said, "Ha! You're a nosey reporter who can't stay out of other people's business. If you'd taken our advice, then you wouldn't be in this mess."

She straightened in her chair and said with defiance, "What you're doing is wrong. You're stealing Indian heritage and that's not right."

"You think that matters to me? You're crazy, lady."

"One of these days, you'll get caught," she warned. "I'll report you to the authorities!"

Johnson guffawed as if she had said something ridiculous. Just then he felt a hand clamp down firmly on his shoulder. As he turned around to see who it was, he felt a powerful blow to his face, right between the eyes. A sharp pain pierced through his head and his eyes became blurry.

John had been hiding behind the tall stack of boxes. While Julia kept the burly man's attention, he was able to sneak up behind him without a sound. After smacking the enemy in his face, he hooked hard to the jaw and sent the man's head whipping to the side. With an uppercut to the chin, the burly man's head jerked backwards. Then John spread his feet for balance, and with a powerful right punch to the belly, the burly man bent over in pain and groaned. To finish him off, or put him out of his misery, John quickly slid his revolver from its holster and bonked the man on the head. He tumbled to the ground without a sound.

John grabbed the man's Macarov from its holster and stuffed it in the small of his back behind his belt. Quickly, he pulled out his pocketknife and strode over to Matthew. He bent down and cut the twine off his wrists and then his ankles. As Matthew took off the gag and rubbed the circulation back into his hands, John headed toward Julia.

He knelt down at her feet and looked up into her face. When their eyes met, his heart twisted as he asked with concern, "Did they hurt you, Sweetheart? Are you all right?"

She smiled and nodded, not trusting herself to talk. She knew she would weep, just out of gratefulness for her husband.

John cut the twine from her wrist and then he brought her hand to his lips and tenderly kissed her palm, feeling grateful she was all right.

As he cut her feet loose, she stroked his hair with her hand and said softly, "Hey! You need an old, beat-up hat."

"What?"

"You remind me of Indiana Jones saving the day."

John's eyes crinkled at the corners as he smiled at her and said softly, "Not for long. Let's get outta here before the head Nazi arrives."

"Devollyn? He's gone to town."

"How about his henchmen?" John asked as he stood and looked toward the door with wariness.

"You've got a point there. I'm ready when you are," she said as she slowly rose from the hard, rickety chair and rubbed the soreness from her backside. That chair had kept her prisoner much too long. Before John could stop her, she headed toward the small room that held the antiquities.

"Julia? We don't have much time. What's up?"

"I've got to get something first."

She quickly ran into the small room, grabbed the pendant, and stuffed it in her pocket. There was no way she was going to let these men take off with it. It had a special significance and she knew it. She felt it deep inside.

As she ran out of the room, John led them toward the back door where he had entered. Then all three of them took off up the slope to safety ... or wherever safety was. John was not sure where that was at this moment.

They wound their way southward toward the mouth of the canyon, stopping and listening every now and then for any signs of the enemy.

Chapter 22

After following the back road up the mountain for a ways, Matthew asked, "Which way should we go? They're all over the place looking for you."

Julia had a look of concern as she exclaimed, "What about the artifacts? They're taking off tomorrow morning, and they'll get away with everything. We've got to stop them."

John's eyes widened with disbelief. "What are you talking about, Julia? From my last count, there's twelve of them and only three of us. What can we do?"

"I don't know. I just think we should stop them somehow."

"How? Tell me and I'll do it," he blurted out in an irritated tone.

Julia shrugged, ignoring his impatience. She knew he was feeling stressed.

Realizing how sharp he had been, John calmed down and apologized, "I'm sorry, but I'm frustrated over this whole incident."

She nodded.

"How about this? We'll find a safe spot to hide and then we'll think about it. Maybe we can come up with a plan. In the meantime, our lives are in danger. They want us dead because we know too much."

As they sat on a log resting and discussing the situation, they heard the crunching of twigs and limbs and before they had a chance to take cover, they heard a man yell from a distance, "There they are!"

The henchmen were quite a ways off, but John instantly stood and grabbed Julia's hand and took off, with Matthew following close behind. Bullets began flying every which way, and Julia felt a bullet whiz past her like the sound of a buzzing bee. She gasped in terror and her heart picked up speed, pumping adrenaline through her veins.

"This way," John yelled as he let go of her hand and headed up the side of the mountain.

He was hoping to make it more difficult for the men to follow. The junipers could shield and protect them while the rocky mountainside would slow the men down. If the way was tough, then they might give up. Besides that, he knew it was difficult to shoot uphill. Because of elevation, it makes the angle deceiving. This was their only chance, and they had to take it.

The juniper trees were thick, and the sagebrush was meshed tightly together, making it difficult to pass through. They steadily worked their way through the desert brush and growth, hurrying at a quick pace. As they hiked between the junipers, Julia's arms began stinging from being scratched by sharp limbs that were in her way, but she did not complain.

After a while, they finally came to a barren side of the mountain where a few rugged cliffs rose upward. The junipers became scarce along the rocky area, but the steep rocky mountain would be hard for the henchmen to keep up.

There was not much of a breeze, but it helped a little

as the sun beat down on them. The dampness clung to Julia's skin as the heat bore down on her shoulders and back. Her lungs were burning, but she wearily continued on. When she came upon thick layers of flat rocks, they slid beneath her feet, making Julia stumble and fall several times. She quickly picked herself up and struggled to keep up with John. Out of breath and exhausted, she tried to put one foot in front of the other, telling herself that she could do it.

Matthew was keeping up just fine. He was young and agile and had the stamina for hiking at a quick pace. He was breathing evenly, as if the hike was second nature to him. But Julia was not in condition for such hiking. It took all the adrenaline she had to keep up with the men. She was breathing hard from exhaustion, and her side was throbbing from the constant running and climbing they had done. Julia's head was pounding from all the dust in the air. If they did not stop to rest soon, she would collapse to the ground at any moment.

The enemy was slowly falling behind them, not able to catch up, which made John feel good about his decision. When Julia slipped once again on loose rock, he heard her collapse and fall. John instantly stopped and walked back to help her to her feet.

Noticing her flushed face and heavy breathing, he said with concern, "You need to rest, Julia. You can't go on much further." His eyes searched for a way out of this predicament, and then an idea popped into his mind. "I've got it. That cave I discovered! It's not too far from here. If we can reach it, then we'll be out of sight, and they won't know which direction we took."

Julia nodded in agreement and rubbed her sore, dusty hands on her pant legs. Then she followed John, climbing toward the cave. It was another five minutes, but they were able to make it without anyone seeing where they went. John pushed the overhanging branches away from the cave so Julia could walk in. She only made it a couple of feet before she collapsed to the ground. Her legs were trembling and her breathing was uneven. She felt ragged. Her face was bright red and her back was soaked with sweat.

"Not here, Julia. Just a little further inside where they can't see us."

Julia slowly shook her head. "No, John. I can't move. I can't go any further."

John understood and sat down beside her and let her rest for a few minutes. Her chest was rising and falling with each breath she took, and he could tell that he had pushed her a little too far.

Matthew's face was damp with sweat. He wiped it with his sleeve as he found a place to rest against the wall of the cave. He closed his eyes and tried to relax.

Sweat was beading up and rolling down the small of John's back and his brow was dripping. He pulled his handkerchief out and swiped at his forehead. His damp shirt clung to his body, exposing the muscles rippling along his chest and accentuating his broad shoulders. John looked at his bedraggled wife and wrapped his arm around her and pulled her head on his shoulder so she could relax for a few minutes.

As John looked around at the tunnel, thoughts of worry intruded his mind. What if the men found this cave? What if they decided to search it? If they did, the men could easily surround them and they could be trapped. Besides that, if there were to be a confrontation, would the men allow them to live? Was it a bad idea to even come here? The dread that he felt at that moment made his mind work feverishly to conjure up another plan. He had his .357 Magnum and the Macarov. Therefore, they were not totally defenseless.

After fifteen minutes had passed, Julia's breathing was not so labored and began to even out. He could tell that she was about ready to get up and go deeper into the cave.

Just at that moment, Matthew perked up his ears and whispered, "Did you hear that? They're getting closer. They've caught up to us, John."

John helped Julia to her feet and they started back through the tunnel. Suddenly, he stopped. An idea came to his mind. He turned around and eyed the entrance of the cave and the way it was built. If they decided to check the cave out, he had an idea that would stop their searching all together.

Matthew whispered with anxiety, "They're almost here. What should we do?"

"I've got an idea. Let's hide here where the tunnel curves. It's dark enough to hide us but close enough to do what I've got planned just in case they come in."

"But … uh…" stammered Julia. "How could they find this place? Junipers surround the entrance."

John slid his revolver out of its holster and then knelt down on the ground, resting his hand on his knee. Matthew and Julia huddled together against the wall in the shadows of the cave and waited, wondering what John had planned. It did not take long until a group of men stopped near the entrance to rest.

One man said in a breathless tone, as if exhausted, "Do ya think they came this way?"

"Dunno. Not sure. They just seemed to disappear."

Another man had been resting against a bunch of branches. Thinking the rock wall was solid behind him, he leaned his weight into it and the limbs seemed to give way. Realizing the canyon wall was not solid, he turned around with curiosity. As he peered through the darkness, he instantly stood erect.

He moved in closer and peeked inside the cave and asked, "Hey, what about this cave? Do ya think they'd come in here to hide?"

"What cave?" asked the leader.

"This one," he said as he pointed through the branches. "Let's check it out. Do you have a flashlight?"

"Naw."

The leader yelled to the rest of the men who were approaching and breathing heavily, "Any of you have a flashlight?"

One man slowly walked toward him, looking peaked and breathing heavily. "I... I do."

He pulled a tiny flashlight from his pocket and handed it to him.

After turning it on, the leader pulled his pistol out of its holster. "The rest of you stay here and guard the entrance. The three of us will go in and check it out."

The owner of the flashlight mumbled something about hating spiders and snakes and preferring to stay outside as guard. While a few of the men chuckled about his dilemma, another man was chosen to accompany the two of them inside the cave. All three men had their pistols drawn as they pushed the branches from the entrance.

John was ready and taking aim at the rotten boards just above the entrance as the men approached the opening of the cave. When the first man began to enter, John let go a blast of shots, one after another, demolishing the rotten beams. The deafening sound of the gunshots penetrated the atmosphere and echoed inside the cave. It did not take much until the entrance began to crumble, collapsing and tumbling to the ground, covering the entrance completely. The cave was pitch dark and dust was flying everywhere.

Matthew was choking from the powdery dust as it settled around him. Julia was in shock at what her husband had just done. She instantly pulled the bottom of her knit shirt over her face so she could breathe. And John had been ready with a red neckerchief. He quickly covered his mouth and nose and waited for the dust to settle.

Linda Weaver Clarke

Chapter 23

"Are you crazy, John?" came an exasperated feminine voice from the dark. "What on earth did you do that for? I've seen you at target practice, so I know you did that on purpose. Why?"

John could tell that Julia was not happy about his little plan and he grinned. He knew that she hated the dark with a passion. That was why they had a night light in their bedroom. So he instantly slid his hand into his pocket, pulled out his flashlight, and flipped it on.

"Yes, I knew exactly what I was doing," he replied calmly.

"Why didn't you just shoot at them and try to scare them away?"

"Scare them away? Are you joking? Nothing would have stopped those men. Greed is their God. Besides, this was better. I thought about it and if I had shot at them in defense, then they would have shot back and someone might have gotten hurt, including me."

"And you thought this was better?" she said in disbelief. "Well, now we definitely won't escape, will we? We'll just stay here and suffocate."

"Now, Julia, have faith in me. I had no other choice, and I knew what I was doing. If we gave ourselves up, they would have taken us prisoner, and then what? We knew too much. They would have had to do away with us. So, I just blasted away at the entrance hoping they'd think I was a bad shot. Now they'll leave us alone, thinking we have no way out."

"That's right. Now this cave is holding us prisoner, instead."

"Didn't you hear me, Julia? I said, they *think* we have no other way out."

Matthew's eyes widened as he asked, "Are you telling me that you know another way out of here?"

"Yup. Remember when I discovered this cave? I did a thorough search of it. It's not so easy to get to, in fact, a little difficult, but it's a way out."

"What do you mean not so easy?" Julia asked.

"Well, it's a climb and it's narrow. But we can do it."

Julia sat in silence, and her thoughts began to stray. There was no sign of light anywhere, either behind them or in front of them, and Julia became nervous. If the batteries gave out, they would be in utter blackness, and she knew that her eyes would never grow accustomed to this sort of darkness and that was something to fear. Their eyes would be unable to adjust, and the feeling of helplessness and claustrophobia would overtake her.

Nervously, she said, "Uh, John?"

"Yes?"

"Did you put new batteries in your flashlight?"

John could hear the uneasiness in her voice and he smiled. "Of course, I did. Don't worry about a thing."

John scooted toward Matthew and Julia and shined the light on them to see if they were all right. Matthew spat a mouthful of gray saliva on the ground as he looked at

John. His face, hair, and eyebrows were covered with fine dust.

Julia's hair was covered with particles of dirt, but since she had shielded her face with her shirt, she did not look half so bad. And John? Well, he had dust on his eyebrows, upper cheeks, and hair. His neckerchief had only covered his mouth and nose. He was a sight, and Julia giggled when she looked at them.

"What?" asked Matthew.

"If you could see what I see, you'd laugh, too. You're both filthy as can be."

"You're not lookin' so grand yourself, Julia," remarked John as he reached over and plucked a piece of dirt from her hair and showed it to her. "I think you need to wash your hair again. Don't you agree?"

"Hey!" she said in feigned disapproval as she playfully slugged his arm. "If you would have warned me, I could have covered my head as well."

He laughed and then stood up and held his hand out to help her. As she got to her feet, he said, "Follow me."

Then he took her hand and led the way through the cave. After walking a ways through the tunnel, they finally entered the large cavity. John told them to rest before continuing on. Matthew did not care one way or the other, but Julia was glad for the rest. John pulled out his Bic and lit the small candle that sat on the table. He turned off his flashlight to conserve batteries and then settled down on the old chest.

Matthew paced back and forth while Julia sat on one of the chairs. She thought about their situation and began to mull it over in her mind. Finally, an idea came to her.

Julia's eyes brightened as she explained her plan. "I've been thinking and I have an idea. Back at General Steam, I noticed some chairs and logs set around a fire pit that's heaped with ashes."

Matthew stopped pacing and said, "Yes. That's right. When they caught me this morning, they had a large fire going."

"Well, I believe they'll be sitting at the campfire tonight."

John looked curiously at Julia and asked, "What's your point?"

"Well, most people look into the fire as they eat and talk."

"And…"

"They'll lose their night vision. So if we sneak up to them, they won't even see us."

John shook his shook adamantly. "We're not creeping up on anyone, Julia."

"John, just listen to my idea first. Please?"

He nodded. "Go ahead."

"You see, they're going to take off tomorrow morning with all the artifacts, and they'll get away with it. We can stop them if we use a little ingenuity and trickery."

"Like what?" John asked warily.

"You have two pistols. We can fake them out."

"What do you mean?"

"We can trick them into thinking they're surrounded. It's simple. You see, you confront them and tell them to give up."

"Confront them? They aren't dummies. They would challenge me."

"I know, but we can be smarter. Matthew can shoot one pistol and I can wiggle some bushes, making them think there's a bunch of us."

"You haven't thought this through, Julia." He shook his head. "No, we need more than two guns for this sort of trickery. They'll start to wonder why there's wiggling branches on one side of me and shooting on the other side."

"So, we get another gun like you did back there," she said with confidence.

John chuckled at her positive attitude. "You're so cute, Julia. You think it'll be that easy again? That was just a fluke. Besides, you helped distract him, and that made a big difference."

"I can distract someone else…"

He chuckled again. "Not on your life. I'm not putting you into danger."

"How about me?" asked Matthew.

John shook his head. "I've got to think this through first."

Julia smiled charmingly, as if that would make a difference, and said, "All right, let's play it by ear and see what happens. If it doesn't work, then we'll go to plan B."

John grinned. "So, what's plan B?"

"Run for our lives. It's dark. We'll have our night vision on our side."

John tried so hard to suppress another chuckle as he said, "You've been doing quite a bit of thinking about this, haven't you?"

"Sure have."

"How do you know it'll work?"

"I read it in a Louis L'Amour book."

How he treasured her! She was so sure of herself. Seeing her like this made him admire her strong will, and he just wanted to squeeze her tight. She was so adorable when she came up with ideas. It was as if she really had faith that it would work. Was she right, though? Could they do it? It sounded too easy.

Rising from his seat, John asked, "Do you want to see the hole I found that we can climb through?"

Both Matthew and Julia nodded.

He turned on his pocket flashlight and blew out the candle. Then he led the way to a narrow passage and shined the light on the walls and ceiling of the tunnel. It looked solid, and that was a comfort to everyone.

They worked their way deeper into the cave, winding around bends until the tunnel finally straightened out. After a while, they saw a stream of light ahead of them. As they approached, Julia could see sunshine and tree roots cascading down through a large hole in the ceiling.

"When I found this," said John, "I wondered if maybe the rain created this hole, and each time it rained, it simply got bigger."

"But…" Julia looked at her husband. "How do we get out?"

"You climb up one of these roots."

John grinned as he pulled on a large root that was sticking through the hole and looked at Matthew. "Do you want to try it and see if it'll hold you?"

"Be glad to," he said with confidence.

Matthew was athletic and for him this was a simple task to perform. He grabbed a root and yanked on it to see if it was sturdy. Then he pulled himself upward, one arm at a time. The muscles in his biceps flexed as he pulled himself closer and closer toward the ceiling. Just as he got to the top, he stuck his hand out of the hole.

"Good," said John. "Now come on down. I think we should give it another hour or so just in case there's still someone walking around. We want them to think we're buried in the cave."

Matthew nodded, slid down the large root with his feet clasped tightly around it, and landed with a thump on the ground.

Julia folded her arms and said doubtfully, "So how do you expect me to get out of this hole? I don't have the same strength as you two."

"I already have that figured out. Matthew will go up first, then I'll have you stand on my shoulders, and he'll grab your arms and pull you through the hole."

Julia nodded. "It might work. What shall we do in the meantime?"

He shrugged. "We could go back and relax for a while."

"Or…" she said with curiosity, eyeing the dark tunnel where it continued on. "We could see where this takes us."

"I'm for that," said Matthew without hesitation.

John nodded. "Sounds good to me."

They only walked a few feet when they came upon a steep decline. John shined his light downward to the lower level. There were some chiseled steps in the rock surface, descending into a room, and the sunlight shining from the hole gave enough light to see their way downward. Carefully, they took one step at a time until they got to the bottom. As they entered the large cavity, John heard the sound of dripping water. Squatting on his heels, he examined the wet ground. He followed the wetness with his flashlight and found a few shallow pools where water was dripping from a crack.

"Anyone thirsty?"

"I am," said Julia with relief.

She knelt down and cupped her hands in the fresh spring water and sipped. After she drank her fill, Matthew knelt down for a drink. John stood silently waiting his turn, allowing the flashlight to play on the ceiling and walls. Then his eyes widened in astonishment as he took a deep breath. He had never seen such a magnificent sight in his whole life. Had this been an Anasazi dwelling?

Chapter 24

John had read about Indian caves in magazines. Some were found in Montana and others in Florida. Bones and shards had been found and even rock art, but this was phenomenal. He slowly walked to the wall, feeling a sense of reverence.

"It's a rock art panel," John informed the others.

"Wow!" said Matthew. "I've never seen something like this before."

"A panel like this is something you don't see very often," said John as he stared in awe. "It's full of Native American artwork, which tells a story about their tribe. Archaeologists have learned their lifestyle, beliefs, customs, and everyday life through rock art."

"I haven't seen petroglyphs like this before," said Julia. "They aren't petroglyphs. It's a pictograph."

"What's the difference?"

"A petroglyph has images carved on the surface of black desert varnish. A pictograph uses paint such as red, orange, and green." He pointed to an image. "See these handprints? They're pictographs."

Julia moved in closer for a better look.

Matthew drew his brows together with curiosity and

asked, "How did they do it?"

"By pressing pigment-covered hands against the wall. They're called stamped handprints." Pointing to other prints, he added, "These over here are negative handprints. You place your hands on the wall and blow pigment on top of your hands. So, what you see is the handprint with color surrounding it."

Julia laughed. "Reminds me of stencils on a wall. How did you learn so much about handprints?"

"From Paul. You don't mingle with archaeologists without learning a bunch. I ask plenty of questions, too." John pointed to some brown pictographs, and his eyes widened with excitement. "Here's a harvest scene. I've never seen such detailed art before. See here? A father is throwing seeds in the air while his family is working the soil. And there's a bird flying above them in the air."

The wonderment he felt was unlike anything he had experienced before. The ambiance in this cave was positive. John had learned that a Native American "sacred place" was a place that had no alterations done to it and had not been desecrated by humans in any way. A feeling of reverence came over him as he marveled at the scene.

Julia felt it, too, as she pointed toward another scene. A man was holding his child's hand, and his wife was expecting a baby. She had a round belly and inside was a small figure of a person.

With excitement in her voice, she said, "I wonder if her husband drew this, telling the history of his family."

John put his arm around her shoulder as they eyed the pictograph. When he heard Julia gasp, he turned toward her and saw her pointing at a pendant hanging around the woman's neck. It had red and black beads with a red triangle pendant. Julia dug into her pocket. She gently pulled the necklace out and dangled it from her hand.

John aimed the flashlight on the pendant and took a closer look as he rubbed his chin with curiosity. "Well, I'll be. Where did you find this?"

"At General Steam. That's what I went after when you untied me."

"We'll make sure that Paul puts this in a museum with the Anasazi artifacts."

As Julia stared at the little family on the wall, an overwhelming impression came into her soul, and at that very moment, she knew this necklace was a gift from this woman's husband. She bore his child and this was a symbol of his eternal love for her. And to protect it, she put it in a pot.

Julia turned toward her husband and said, "You're right. We must put it in a museum along with their story. This scene tells of a family, their harvest, and their love for one another. It's their legacy, their heritage."

John nodded as he gazed at the scene before him. "Yes, their legacy."

Julia knew that she would never forget this day, standing in a place where an ancient people once lived and holding a part of the past in her hand. Later, she would explain her feelings to John. But right now, she wanted to relish this moment. She carefully tucked the necklace in her pocket and stood a while in thought.

Matthew walked toward a figure and grimaced as he said, "Here's someone holding a snake in his hand."

John walked toward him and smiled. "A snake isn't a bad

symbol, Matthew. It's a spiritual symbol."

"How can a snake be spiritual?"

"It's an ancient Indian legend. There were two serpents in paradise, one was a good serpent and the other was a bad serpent. The bad one represented Lucifer while the good serpent represented the creator of the earth." John pointed toward the painting and said, "That man is holding a spiritual symbol."

"You mean, they believed in Christ?"

"Well, they have a different name for him. They called him Maasaw."

Julia scanned the wall and said, "At least this rock art isn't defaced since no one knows about it."

"Such as people carving their initials on the wall?" Matthew asked.

John nodded. "I found some art panels that were used as targets with bullet holes all over it."

He sighed heavily, wishing people had more respect for the ancient past. John knelt beside the small pool of water and sipped until he was satisfied and asked, "Want another drink before we head back?"

Julia nodded. As she bent over, she felt a slight movement of air across her cheeks, coming from the opposite end of the tunnel.

She looked up and asked, "Can you feel that?"

John knelt beside her. After a while, he nodded. "Follow me. Let's see where the breeze is coming from. It's probably another opening like the one we just found. Maybe it'll be easier to climb through."

As John headed deeper into the tunnel, Matthew looked a little concerned and asked, "Are you sure it's safe, not a dead end or something?"

"It couldn't be. We both felt a breeze in this direction."

As they walked through the tunnel, the breeze became stronger and they stopped and looked around.

"Perhaps it's coming from the ceiling like the other opening," said Matthew.

John pointed the flashlight toward the ceiling but found nothing.

As Julia walked around her husband, looking upwards, she felt her foot begin to slide from beneath her. She gasped. Throwing her arms in the air, Julia screamed. She felt herself slide downwards. She tried to grab something, anything she could. But it was to no avail. Unbridled terror swept over her. Her heart pounded against her ribs as she felt herself begin to fall into the chasm below.

Linda Weaver Clarke

Chapter 25

Julia's heart sank as she felt herself sliding into the depths beneath her. As she screamed, Julia felt someone grab onto her arm and hold tightly. As she dangled in the air, her heart pounded furiously and an overwhelming fear overtook her like a stabbing pain in the chest.

She was breathing heavily when she heard John's calming voice tell her, "Julia, I've got you. Just relax or I won't be able to get you out. You've got to stop wiggling. Work with me, all right?"

Julia whimpered as she dangled helplessly in the air. Then she said, "Wh-what do you want me to do?"

"Julia, hand me your other arm. It might be easier to pull you out."

She tried to raise her arm upward, but fear seemed to be working against her. It would not budge, lying limply at her side.

"I can't. I can't move it."

"Just try harder, Julia. It's all right. I've got hold of you. Stop panicking. Try lifting your other arm towards me. I'm waiting."

"H-how deep is this hole, John?"

"Julia, you don't want to know. Now hand me your other

arm, all right?"

With that answer, she gasped. "John? Am I dangling in an abyss?"

"Your arm, Julia, and then I'll answer that," he said gently, hoping to calm her down with a deep soothing tone.

With great concentration, Julia slowly raised her arm above her head. When she felt John grab hold of her other arm, she breathed a sigh of relief.

He gradually pulled her onto solid ground, her legs still dangling through the hole. Then he tucked his hands under Julia's arms to get a better grip and said, "Now, to answer your question. Well, Julia, I can't see the bottom. Does that classify as an abyss?"

"O-o-oh, my! It does," she whimpered as she felt herself slowly being pulled over the edge of the hole.

As John pulled her body to a safer place next to the wall, he playfully grunted and moaned in feigned exhaust.

Julia leaned back against it and then looked at John sitting beside her and slapped his shoulder. "That's for grunting and moaning."

He chuckled.

Then she leaned against his chest and hugged him. "Thanks, John."

"What? Is that all a hero gets for saving a fair maiden?" John said teasingly. "A hit and a hug? I do believe that Indiana Jones got more than that for saving the girl. And how about Brendan Fraser in *The Mummy*? And Crocodile Dundee?"

Julia laughed. "I don't believe that Crocodile Dundee would have groaned and moaned when saving a woman. I'm not sure about Brendan Fraser, though. He might, just to get a row out of her."

John grinned. He loved getting her goat. As they leaned against the wall, he felt another cool, soft breeze touch his sweaty face.

"Did you feel that?" John asked.

"Yes," answered Matthew. "It's coming from the tunnel."

John leaned over and held his hand above the hole, but there was nothing. He held his hand toward the tunnel and felt the breeze come from that direction. He smiled and reached for his flashlight that had fallen to the ground in the attempt to save Julia. Then he got to his feet and checked out their situation. Noticing a two-foot ledge between the hole and the wall, he put pressure on it with his foot. It was firm solid rock.

John turned toward the others and said, "The breeze is coming from that direction, and I think this tunnel comes out that way."

"But the hole," said Julia cautiously.

"This ledge is solid rock. Don't worry. We'll be able to make it." John led the way and walked across the narrow ledge with no trouble. "It's not bad. Just be careful and don't look down."

Julia was next. Facing the rock wall, she slid her feet across, taking one step at a time. She took another step and another, sliding her feet carefully inch by inch. When she felt John grab her tightly around the arm, she breathed a sigh of relief.

After she stepped on solid ground, he said, "Now it's your turn, Matthew."

He shook his head adamantly. "I'm afraid of heights, John. I can't do it."

"I understand completely. I'm the same way, but I know you can do it."

"No! I think I'll go back and climb through the hole."

"Matthew, what's the difference from this hole and the other one?"

He looked down into the hole and frowned. "I know there's a bottom to that one."

"I see." John rubbed his chin as he thought. "Matthew, do you see that ridge on the side of the wall?"

"Yes."

"Good. Don't look down. Just grab onto the ridge with both hands as you move across. It'll help balance you. When you get close enough, I'll grab hold of your arm and help you off the ledge. Now don't worry. It's solid and part of the floor. You can do it."

He handed Julia his flashlight. Then he leaned toward the ledge and held his hand out toward Matthew as a gesture of confidence.

"Come on, Matthew. You can do it. Just slide your feet across a few steps at a time."

Matthew stared at John's hand and then decided to try it. He held onto the protruding ridge with both hands and then slid his foot across the rock ledge. After a few more steps, he felt John's hand clamp tightly around his arm, squeezing it to reassure him.

"Just a couple more steps and you've got it, Matthew."

He breathed in deeply and slid his feet across.

"One more step," said John reassuringly.

Matthew held on tight as he slid his foot across. Just at that moment, the ridge broke and crumbled in his hand, causing him to lose his balance. As he gasped, he felt John tighten his grip around his arm and yank him toward solid ground. As he fell into John's arms, his heart was pounding like no other. The anxiety that rose within him was indescribable. All he wanted to do was weep.

With tears stinging his eyes, Matthew stammered, "N-never! I'm never doing that again."

"That's all right with me, Matthew," John said as he held him tightly in his arms, trying to comfort the frightened young man.

When Matthew's heart slowed down, he straightened and said, "For a moment there, I thought I was a goner. I'm never doing that again, and no one's talking me into it, either."

"Hopefully," said John, "there won't be a next time."

"Now I understand how April feels."

"April?" asked John.

"Yeah. She's got a real phobia for height. I never realized how real her fears were until right now."

John nodded as he took the flashlight from his wife. After Matthew got his breath back, they continued on. They came upon several crosscuts, some old rusted carts, and a bank with some ore chutes.

When he heard a hammering sound in the distance, John stopped and held his hand up and whispered, "Did you hear that?"

Everyone nodded. After a few moments, he continued on with more caution. As Julia followed, she began to feel a growing sense of uneasiness. They had not gone very far when they heard the pounding once again. After walking a few more yards, they rounded a corner and saw a hint of light and heard the murmur of voices in the distance. John immediately shut off the flashlight and shoved it into his pocket. Silently, they crept at a slower pace and then stopped when the voices were more audible.

"Just give up, will ya," came a crusty voice from the distance.

"I can't. I know there's more gold here. If I find it, then I'll be rich."

"There isn't enough gold here for all the work you're doin'. Can't you get it through your thick skull, Fred? This was just a cover, just in case someone came poking around like that stupid reporter."

"All the good that did," Fred growled. "If it wouldn't have been for that bumbling foreman who poisoned those cats, then that nosy reporter wouldn't have figured anything out. Those cats did no harm."

"Hey, I wouldn't be talking if I were you. You were the one that picked them up, feeding them and encouraging those mangy cats to stay."

"I like cats. They might have gotten killed by coyotes."

Hidden in the shadows, John inched his way toward the men and peeked around the corner. He saw a man bent over with a pick in his hand while another was standing at his side.

"Well, you're wasting your time. I'm not doing this anymore," the crusty man said in frustration. "By the way, a few of us are leaving in half an hour. If you're not down from this cave by then, you'll have to come with the others in the morning, and you'll have to ride in the back of the truck with the artifacts, if that's your choice."

"What others?" asked Fred. "I thought we were leaving tomorrow."

"Devollyn changed his mind, said that we're going to Vegas tonight while his foreman and a couple others take the truck out in the morning. It's too dark for the truck to leave now. He's afraid we'll hit too many bumps and hurt some of those valuable relics. Johnson knows what to do. He's done it before. So, are ya comin' or staying?"

"Not sure. I'm going to work a little longer."

"Remember, Fred, if you're not down and ready to go, we're leaving."

He turned on his heels and stomped out, leaving his partner behind.

John tiptoed back to the others and whispered, "Did you hear that? They're leaving only three men to drive the truck out. I've got an idea. Matthew, will you walk out there and say something to the man kneeling on the ground? While you distract him, I'll get him from behind."

"What should I say?"

"Hmmm, something intelligent. That should confuse him good."

Matthew grinned at his sense of humor and then asked with concern, "Is he armed?"

"Naw. I don't think so. I didn't see anything." Matthew smiled. "All right then. I'll do it."

He crept up to the opening, trying to think of something intelligent to say and then walked out nonchalantly and asked, "Do you happen to have the time?"

The man did not look up but looked at his watch and answered, "It's pert-near…" He squinted at his watch. "I don't have my glasses. Tell 'em I'll be through after a while."

"Did you find much gold here?"

"Naw," he said as he turned around.

When he saw Matthew standing before him, his eyes widened. Before he could react, John had his gun pushed up against his back and told him to stay where he was. Then he snatched the pistol from the man's holster and told Matthew to tie him up with the twine that was hanging over a cart.

Matthew's eyes were wide as he stared at John. "I thought you said he wasn't armed."

"Well, I didn't see anything when I peeked around the corner."

"And I thought you were going to hit him from behind so I wouldn't get hurt."

"Well, when I saw the twine, I changed my mind. Why give a man a headache when we can tie him up and gag him. Besides, he loves cats. I couldn't help it."

"What?" Matthew said incredulously.

"He likes cats. That's one point for him. Now hurry. It's almost dark and we need to find our way down this mountain." John smiled at Julia and said, "We've got another gun here. I think we could work out that plan of yours after all."

Matthew was tying the prisoner when he turned around in surprise. "Think so?"

"Yup."

John handed the pistol to Julia. He took the other pistol from the small of his back and handed it to Matthew. Then he gagged their prisoner.

Matthew looked at Julia in surprise and pointed at the pistol in her hand. "Can Julia shoot?"

"Can she shoot? Son, I take her out target shooting with me every now and then. She's quite good."

"What are we going to do with him?" said Matthew as he pointed to Fred.

"I'll come back with the authorities tonight and pick him up."

Linda Weaver Clarke

Chapter 26

By the time they got to the bottom of the mountain, it was dark. They walked silently toward the mining community and saw the bonfire in full array. Three men were clinking coffee cups and eating as they talked among themselves.

As John stealthily crept forward, Julia's stomach growled and he stopped in mid-step. She looked up when he turned to face her. He put a finger to his lips as she touched her stomach with a guilty look on her face.

"What? I'm hungry," Julia whispered. "I haven't eaten since breakfast."

"Just so they don't hear us sneaking up on 'em," he said with a smile.

They crept among the shrubs, not too far from the fire, and then separated, each finding a perfect place to hide and await John's signal.

After giving Julia and Matthew plenty of time to hide, John took a deep breath, gave a little prayer inside, and then yelled, "You're surrounded. Don't move an inch or we'll start shooting."

The foreman instantly stood with his plate in hand and peered out toward the shrubbery, trying to see who was calling to them while the other two men froze where they sat. As the fire lit up his face, John could see that his nose was puffy and swollen. He also noticed that the man was ready to draw his gun at any moment, so John decided to give him a warning.

Aiming carefully, he shot the foreman's tin plate from his hand and yelled, "I said to not move an inch, didn't I?"

Johnson was so startled that he dared not move again. He stood still and yelled out, "Who are you? I don't believe we're surrounded or you'd show your faces."

At that moment, Julia shot a log that was protruding from the bonfire, and the flames danced and sparkled as the bullet disturbed the atmosphere. It shaved off small pieces of wood and took fire and began sizzling. The three men instantly turned toward the fire and realized that was a warning for them to cooperate.

Matthew's eyes widened when he realized how good Julia was. He also knew that was his signal to do something, so he took careful aim at a jug lying on the ground. But instead of hitting it, he accidentally shot the tip of the man's shoe a couple of feet from the jug. He was sitting on a log and it startled him good.

The man instantly jumped to his feet, dropped his coffee cup to the ground, and yelled, "I believe ya. Don't shoot. I believe ya."

Matthew's eyes widened. How could his aim be so far off? Quickly, he moved to a different spot and waited.

John yelled, "That was just a warning. Drop your firearms and stand facing the fire. Then put your hands on the back of your heads."

Johnson became suspicious, drew his revolver, and yelled, "Who are ya? FBI? Police? I don't think we're surrounded at all. Why would you hide if you had a lot of men? We're only three people and you could take us easy if you had as many as you say. Why would we shoot back, knowing we were outnumbered? I think you're that Mr. Evans."

One of the men said cautiously, "No, it can't be. I saw him shoot the sides of the cave and he got himself buried."

"No, it's him all right. He got out."

"But what if you're wrong?"

"I'm not." Taking a chance, Johnson yelled, "We can take you easy. How'd you get outta that cave, anyway?"

The men began to stir, wondering if their foreman was right. They slid their hands toward their holsters, ready for action. As they mumbled to one another, John realized that he needed to do something quick before it got out of hand. He needed to intimidate them. So he shot at the jug that Matthew had missed, and it toppled to the ground.

That was the signal Matthew and Julia were waiting for. Now it was their turn. Julia hit the stump, which the third man was sitting on, and made him jump in the air.

Poor Matthew tried to shoot at a log in the fire like Julia had, hoping it was safer since his object was much larger, but he missed. Instead of hitting the log, he hit a man's hat from his head, and it went flying through the air into the fire. It immediately took flame and sizzled away.

The man's eyes widened as he complained, "That's my good hat." Then he looked at the foreman and said gruffly, "I think we ought to listen to him. I think there's a lot more than we realize out there. They mean business."

"Don't listen to him. He won't shoot us. He wouldn't want to have blood on his hands."

John yelled once more, "Throw your weapons to the ground and face the fire with your hands behind your heads. If anyone turns away from the fire, I will take it as a threat to my life, and I will have my posse shoot without questions. Got it?"

The two men immediately agreed to the terms and tossed their pistols to the ground. When Johnson saw how easily his men were intimidated, he cursed and tossed his gun as well. Then they turned toward the fire with their hands behind their heads.

John knew his wife was right about not having their night vision, so he meandered toward the men with confidence. He had the twine from the cave hanging over his shoulder. John slid his gun into its holster, pulled out his pocketknife, and cut a few long strands of twine. Then he pulled the arms of one man down and bound his wrists tight. He went to the next two men and did likewise.

Curiosity got to the men and they turned around to see how many there were. It took a while for their eyes to adjust to the darkness, and then a groan was heard as the men focused on Julia and Matthew. Johnson scowled and mumbled a few curses, condemning his men for giving up so easily.

While Matthew gathered up the weapons, Julia quickly walked to her husband and said, "John, ask him where their boss went. We know that he's in Las Vegas, but where in Vegas?"

John eyed the men as he asked each one where their boss had gone, but no one said a word. He turned to the burly foreman. His nose was black and blue and he looked a sight.

"Where's your boss?" John demanded.

Johnson glared at him with hatred, remembering what John had done to him.

He smiled at the foreman and said, "Too bad about your nose. Didn't mean to mess you up that bad. Now are you going to cooperate or not?"

Johnson pursed his lips tightly, looked away, and would not say a word. So John figured that it was up to the authorities to take care of it. He led the men to the back of the truck. As he waited for each one to climb inside, he looked at Matthew and smiled.

"I didn't know you were such a good shot, Matthew. I'll have to take you target shooting with me next time."

Matthew gave a crooked smile, trying to hide his nervousness at such an offer. "Thanks, but I think I'll pass."

Matthew did not want to shame himself in front of John, and besides, he did not like guns in the first place. He abhorred them. The only reason he went along with the plan was because of the artifacts.

When the last man climbed in, Matthew shut the metal doors and pulled the iron clasp down into the slot, locking it up tight. Then John hopped in the driver's side of the cab while the others climbed in the passenger side.

"Hey, John," said Matthew. "Where are we taking these varmints?"

"To the police department. Then we'll get in touch with Paul and have him press charges. He knows the laws concerning vandalism. Also, he's knowledgeable about who's in charge of the archaeology goings-on here."

"How about Devollyn?"

"He escaped. There's nothing we can do about it. I don't even think that's his real name, so it'll be difficult finding him.

I'm sure the FBI will do something, but we don't have much to go on."

After Julia settled in the middle seat, John asked Matthew, "Do you have the keys?"

"What keys?"

"To the truck. We can't go anywhere without keys, you know."

Matthew's foot slipped on the step of the truck and his eyes widened. "I don't have the keys."

"But I thought you were supposed to search the foreman to see if he had the keys on him."

"But you didn't tell me to," he said frantically. "Now what are we going to do? I suppose you'll make me go back and search him."

John shook his head and turned to his wife, "Naw. We'll have Julia do that."

She grimaced. "The way he looked at me? I wouldn't touch him with a ten foot pole." She poked John in the ribs and he chuckled. "Now stop teasing poor Matthew. He's had enough for one day. I saw you take the keys from the foreman's pocket after tying his hands."

John pulled the keys from his pocket and laughed when he saw Matthew's eyes jerk toward them. "Hop in, Matthew. Let's head out."

As Matthew climbed in beside Julia, he slammed the door shut and asked, "How do you put up with such a man, Julia?"

She laughed softly. "It's not easy, Matthew. Not easy at all. If you only knew how much I have to endure!"

John started the truck, turned toward Julia in feigned disappointment, and said, "What kind of remark was that?"

She laughed.

John cleared his throat dramatically and asked, "So, have you learned anything from this little episode, Mrs. Evans?" When she looked puzzled by his statement, he prompted, "Have you learned to trust your husband a little more, such as listening to my advice?"

"What do you mean?"

"I warned you about this assignment when you told me about the note, but you wouldn't listen. You have to realize that I'm wise and a trustworthy fellow."

Julia smiled, trying to hold back a snicker. "Trustworthy?"

"You bet!"

"Just like the Boy Scouts, huh?" She kissed his cheek and said, "Talking about trustworthy, did you know that the divorce rate in the world is more than fifty percent? But if you've earned your Eagle Scout Award, the rate is much lower?"

John shook his head in confusion. Bewildered was more like it. Where in heaven's name did that come from? What did that have to do with trusting one's husband? She always skipped from one subject to another, and he couldn't seem to keep up with her.

He lifted an eyebrow in puzzlement and said, "Yeah. But what does that have to do with being trustworthy? You've lost me again."

"Well, just like that spaghetti string I was telling you about. When you said trustworthy, it reminded me of the Boy Scout motto, and that reminded me of the Eagle Scout Awards, and that reminded me of this magazine article I read, which reminded me of the divorce rate."

Feeling even more confused, he blurted out, "I don't follow."

"I recently learned that if a young man earns his Eagle Scout Award, there's less of a chance of getting divorced. Isn't that interesting?"

"What?"

"Yes, it's true. I read the statistics. The scouting program teaches proper respect to others, especially to women and children. The divorce rate among those who received their Eagle Scout Awards is only seven percent. They're better husbands and fathers. Respect is what it's all about." She pointed toward the road. "Let's get going."

John shook his head in bafflement. How did she do that? Julia was a complicated woman to follow, but she made sense. Her little spaghetti string and waffle pocket theory really did make sense after all, but he wouldn't admit it out loud. That's for certain.

John thought about this bit of information she told him and said, "Hmm, did you know that I didn't get my Eagle?"

Julia nodded. "But you're different. You're not the average man."

John grinned as he pushed on the gas and the truck began rolling forward. He could barely keep up with the woman. Julia and her spaghetti strings were quite interesting.

Chapter 27
One Month Later

"I know I should have said this sooner, but thanks for taking care of my parents, Matthew," April said as she rose up on the tips of her toes and gave him a gentle kiss on his cheek.

Matthew flushed a rosy color and said, "Oh, I didn't do much."

"That's not what my dad told me. In fact, he said you're a great shot. He said that your shots scared the living daylights out of those men. If it wouldn't have been for you, they might not have given up because Mom and Dad didn't dare shoot so close for fear of hurting someone."

Not wanting to tell the truth, he just shrugged. "Oh, I'm not that good."

"Hey, don't be so modest. You're a hero." Then she rose up on her toes and gave him another kiss on the other cheek.

That did it! If she realized what those kisses were doing to him, she might have thought twice. Now how could he tell her the truth? If he told her that each shot he made was an accident, would she be disappointed in him? She called him a hero, and her eyes shined as if she was proud of him. What could he say to her?

As he thought about it, what she said was true. His shots

had made a big difference and scared the men out of their wits. So, he did what any young man in love would do. He decided to bask in the glory of her compliments and be a hero. There could be no harm in that. So, he took her by the waist and led her to the door with a Cheshire grin on his face.

April turned toward the hallway and called, "Mom, I'll meet you at the restaurant. We're headed out now. Are you sure you want to wait for Dad? He might be late. You can still come with us."

"Yes, April, I'm sure. I would much rather wait so we can go together. He's been working a lot of late hours this whole month and I love being with your dad. He should be home soon."

"Anything you say. By the way, you have a letter. I put it on the table. It has a Las Vegas postmark."

Matthew opened the door and put his hand on the small of April's back and led her out, shutting the door behind them.

"A Las Vegas postmark?" Julia muttered.

She walked into the kitchen and picked up the envelope and looked at it. It had no return address. She put her thumb under the edge of the envelope and ripped it open. She pulled the letter out and read:

My Dear Mrs. Evans,

You win! I've been in business now for over ten years, and it took a small-town reporter (and a woman to boot) to ruin me. You probably don't realize how many thousands of dollars that you cost me. Well, perhaps we'll meet again some day. Who knows? Good-bye, lovely lady.

Sincerely, alias Devollyn

Julia stared at the letter in disbelief. So, Devollyn was in hiding and his men were taking the punishment. They were behind bars, awaiting trial. The feds had reported that not one of his men knew anything about him or what city he was from or his whereabouts. He was shrewd, cunning, and insightful. She groaned. Julia had given a detailed description of him and hoped that would work. One day he would be caught, and he would pay the price for his selfishness and greed.

Well, she was not about to let it ruin her nice evening. They were invited to dinner by her boss to celebrate the defeat of a notorious corporation and a fantastic article in the newspaper. In fact, they sold more newspapers that week than any other time.

Not only that, she had been promoted to investigative reporter the day before her forty-first birthday. She had accomplished her goal. Life was wonderful! Julia had written about the Santa Clara/Virgin River flooding, told of the faith and charity of the community, discovered looters in the area, and submitted a fantastic story that sold every paper available.

Bill had invited Paul to the celebration dinner since he was in charge of the archaeological sites in the area. Paul had gone through all the artifacts in the truck and helped to distribute them to the Native American Museums for safekeeping. This part of American history would be preserved for future generations.

Julia remembered how elated Paul had been when she handed him the beautiful pendant. He had never seen one that was so well preserved before. It was now safe, along with all the other artifacts.

Since Matthew helped in the capture of the crooks, Bill invited him to dinner, too. He, in turn, asked April if she would accompany him. Julia noticed how April's admiration had risen for Matthew when she told her how brave he had been.

Bill invited Ted to celebrate with them, but he refused to go. He fussed and fumed and said he had a migraine. He hadn't spoken to Julia much or even gone out of his way to greet her since the story in the paper. But Julia could care less.

She smiled and said, "Headache, my foot! Jealousy is more like it. Ted acts like a spoiled kid at times." Then she placed the letter on her desk in the study and waited for John to come home.

After ten minutes of waiting, Julia began pacing the living room floor, first in circles and then in figure eights. This evening, she had decided to dress up in her best dress. She had slipped on an elegant cream-colored dress made of rayon. It was rounded at the neck, had three-quarter length sleeves, and it hung gracefully to her ankles, complementing the soft curves of her figure. She wore simple pearls and silver earrings. She had curled her rich auburn hair under, and it hung softly to her shoulders. Her rosy lips should have turned up at the corners, but they didn't. John was late!

When the back door opened and John walked in, he called, "I'm home. I'll be just a few minutes. I have to shower first, but I won't be long."

John quickly walked to the bathroom, slipped off his clothes, and climbed in the shower. After a two-minute shower, he wiped himself down and then pulled on his clothes.

As he was slipping on his socks, Julia impatiently looked at her watch and said in a discouraged and impatient tone, "O-o-oh, we're going to be so late. I should have gone with April and Matthew after all."

John looked up and smiled. "Why didn't you? Since you knew I'd be late, you could've had a good visit with April and I would have met you there."

"What?"

"I wouldn't have minded."

"You mean it doesn't matter whether we go together?" she said, looking at him incredulously. "I've hardly seen you all month."

"Hey! I'll support anything you choose."

Julia crossed her arms at the waist and frowned. "You don't care whether we go together? That's not very flattering. Personally, I would much rather have heard, 'Oh no, I'm glad you waited. I want to be with you.' But instead you tell me that it doesn't even matter whether we're together or not."

"I didn't mean it that way. I was just being supportive," John said with bewilderment.

"Well, being supportive sometimes can make a woman feel unwanted or like you don't care."

"But I do care." John was now completely confused, wondering what he had said wrong. "I..."

"But it didn't sound like it."

John slid his fingers through his hair in frustration. "Oh man!" He groaned. "Grandpa warned me of days like this."

"Days like what?"

"He said that women give men tests that they're bound to fail."

"I do not," she said defensively, resting her hands on her

hips.

"Just think about it, Julia. You're upset that we're behind schedule, but you knew I would be home late and still chose to go with me. On the other hand, so you wouldn't be late, I encouraged you to go with April this morning, but you refused. Then you accuse me of not wanting to be with you when I'm trying to be supportive. I'm damned if I do and I'm damned if I don't."

Trying hard to look stern, Julia bit her lip to prevent a smile from emerging. As she looked at John, he seemed amused by her attitude, and he smiled at her affectionately. He was right and she knew it. When she noticed the softness in his eyes, she wondered what had come over him. Why was he looking at her in such a way? In actuality, he should be frustrated with her attitude and she knew it.

As John gazed warmly upon her, he realized how lovely she looked. She had gotten all dressed up and was achingly beautiful, even with an "attitude." His eyes slowly swept over her, from head to foot. Julia looked so appealing in her evening gown and the way her hair swept across her face and shoulders. He smiled as he walked toward her and slid his hands around her waist and pulled her close.

"Don't bite your lip, Julia," he said softly. "You think I don't care to be with you? You're wrong. You don't realize how much I think about you at work. I long to be home and hate my long hours. As I ride home, my thoughts are full of you."

The softness in John's eyes and his gentle words touched Julia's heart, and she knew she had been wrong.

He gazed into her eyes and touched her face lovingly. A longing to kiss her rose sharply within him as his eyes trailed down to her mouth. He slid his fingers under her chin and lifted it slightly. Then he pulled her close to his chest with the palm of his hand. John pressed his warm lips to hers, enfolding the softness of her in his arms and caressing her back with love and tenderness.

Julia responded to his affection and wrapped her arms around his neck. As he cradled her in his arms, it seemed as if no one in the world existed but the two of them ... a very familiar feeling. He always knew how to soften her addled senses. And at that very moment, all she knew was John's devoted love as she snuggled into his arms. They were in a world of their own, a world where there were no worries, no clocks, no appointments, just their undeniable love for one another. It was just the two of them. What ecstasy! What bliss!

When Julia's cell phone rang, he knew this was coming to an end. She slowly pulled away, but John immediately pulled her back into his arms again and whispered, "Blast that phone!"

She took a deep breath, trying to get her senses back as he nibbled on her earlobe and down her neck. She swallowed and breathlessly said, "Want to go to Mexico to see the Chichen Itza Ruins?"

John leaned back to look into her face. "What?"

"This afternoon, Bill called. He said the sale of papers went sky high and I deserved a little vacation. What do you think?"

When it finally sunk in, John smiled and said teasingly, "Then it's a date, as long as you leave that darn phone behind."

"Deal. We shouldn't be too late for dinner. Are you ready

to go?"

"As ready as I'll ever be." He pulled her closer and said, "Don't forget where we left off."

"Left off?"

"That's right. We're finishing what we just started when we get home."

Julia's eyes brightened as she nodded. "By the way, I forgot to say thank you."

"For what?"

"For loving me, even when I'm ornery, persistent, and willful."

"No problem! But you forgot stubborn."

She laughed. "Yes, stubborn. Victor Hugo said, 'The supreme happiness of life is the conviction that we are loved; loved for ourselves, or rather, loved in spite of ourselves.'"

"In spite of ourselves?" John grinned. "Does that include cussing?"

"Yes, I believe so."

"Good. Thanks for loving me, in spite of myself."

She smiled back and answered, "It's a pleasure."

"Julia?"

"Yes?"

"You're good for me, you know."

"How?"

"Well, you remind me to be the person I should be. I'll try not to cuss so much from now on."

She controlled the laughter that wanted to bubble out as she said, "I'll believe it when I see it, Mister!"

John laughed as she wiggled out of his embrace and slipped her hand through the crook of his arm. Then they walked out the door, heading for a lovely evening together.

* * *

Excerpt from *Mayan Intrigue*

A Sequel to *The Adventures of John and Julia Evans*

Julia walked out into the cool morning air and breathed in the fresh fragrance. As she slowly strolled down the sidewalk, she thought about her assignment for the *Dixie Chronicle*. She was supposed to write about the ruins of the ancient people of Mesoamerica. What an exciting assignment! She was so thrilled when her boss had given her this important project, the first one he had ever given her since her promotion as an investigative reporter. She smiled with contentment as she walked toward a bunch of tall thick shrubs next to a park.

As Julia stepped around the shrubs, she saw a short pudgy man with wisps of grayish brown hair surrounding his balding head. He was smiling as he admired something in his hand. The man beside him was an unusually tall Latin. His short sleeves revealed his tanned arms and he had dark curly hair that touched the collar of his white shirt.

As the balding man pulled a large envelope from his jacket and handed it to his companion, he exclaimed, "Beautiful! It's simply…"

His words trailed off when his eyes met Julia's. As if startled by her presence, he froze, staring at her with widened eyes.

Instantly, his companion turned around and looked over

his shoulder to see what he was staring at. But it did not take long for the Latin's dark eyes to quickly change from surprise to irritation. Julia noticed that his eyes were hard and cold and his jaw was rigid. A chill went down her spine as a feeling of apprehension crept inside her. Something told her to leave and to leave now. She was not about to question those feelings, so she instantly turned on her heels and strode toward the hotel.

Why had these men acted so strangely? If they had wanted privacy, why did they meet at a public park? But as she thought about it, it was only six o'clock on a Sunday morning. Why would they expect anyone to be wandering through the park at this time of day? What surprised her most was their attitude and the way the Latin had reacted to her presence, as if he were angry.

Feeling uneasy, Julia dared not turn around and see if she was followed but quickly picked up her pace. She quickly strode up the stairs of the hotel and ran headlong into the chest of a man standing near the door.

"Whoa, there, Julia!" Paul said with surprise as he grabbed onto her shoulders. "Why are you in such a hurry? And where's John?"

Feeling startled, it took a few seconds to catch her breath before she could answer. Julia quickly turned around to see if she had been followed, and seeing no one, she sighed with relief.

Paul took her arm and led her to a sofa in the waiting room and sat across from her. "So, what's up? You look as if something's troubling you."

Julia tried to smile reassuringly, but it was more of a forced one instead. "Oh, I was just taking a walk. I couldn't sleep in.

You know, the excitement of being here and all."

Paul smiled back, his eyes full of joy. "I know exactly how you feel, Julia. I couldn't sleep, either. I'm so excited to be here. I really want to thank you for allowing me to come along on this trip. When John told me about your assignment, I just had to invite myself along. This is like a dream come true for me. Man, to be able to see the ruins of Mesoamerica! That's every archaeologist's dream."

Paul was a dear friend who taught at Dixie State College in St. George, Utah. He not only taught American history and archaeology, but he was also a dyed-in-the-wool archaeologist and was constantly involved in restoring the past.

Paul was a serious sort of fellow. He was lean and tall with blond hair and large blue eyes. He had glasses that were set on his long, slender nose, giving him the distinguishing look of a professor. He was thirty-nine years old and still unmarried. As an archaeologist, digging in the dirt was the most exhilarating part of his life and he had not found a woman who could stand digging beside him all day long. Until then, he would remain single.

"So, where's John?" asked Paul with a raise of his eyebrow.

"Still sleeping. I was just headed back to the room to wake him and..." Julia's eyes widened in surprise.

The Latin whom she had seen at the park was standing beside the desk, talking nonchalantly to the clerk and staring straight at Julia. There was no mistake about it. He was the same man, all right. The tall Latin's eyes seemed to penetrate right through her as he smiled but Julia instantly averted her eyes and looked down at her hands lying in her lap. What was he doing here? Had he followed her?

After a moment, she berated herself for being so paranoid. The man probably had a room at the hotel and was just chatting with the clerk. The young boy was very friendly and he had talked with her for some time last night, asking where she was from and so forth.

When she felt Paul touch her hand, she jumped.

"Julia," he said with concern. "What's wrong?"

She leaned toward him and whispered, "I saw two men at the park this morning and something about their conduct gave me the willies."

"What do you mean?"

Julia bit her lip nervously and leaned closer to Paul. "I can't describe it exactly, but inside I have an anxious feeling and I don't know why."

"What are you talking about?"

"He's standing at the desk," she said, keeping her eyes glued on Paul.

He turned toward the front desk and asked with puzzlement, "Who? The desk clerk?"

"No, the other one."

"There isn't anybody else, Julia."

She looked up toward the desk and saw the clerk busily working. "He's gone."

"Shall I ask the clerk about this man? If he's bothering you, we should report it."

Julia shook her head, feeling ridiculous. "Oh, it's nothing. I'm just being paranoid in a strange land." She stood and gestured toward the dining room. "I'll see you in about an hour for breakfast."

Author's Notes

I always enjoy putting a little history in my novels. Using fictional characters, I based my story on the Santa Clara/Virgin River flood in St. George, Utah, in 2005. The information about the flooding is accurate. The whole episode was a complete disaster, where many lost their homes to the raging river, including their belongings and photos of the past. Concerned citizens in the area put the Muddy River Fund-Raiser together. The final total earned was $26,765. The experience of charity, love, and caring by everyone in the area was so incredible. There was no prejudice of religion, race, culture, or status, just unconditional love and caring for everyone.

The woman whose Book of Remembrance was found said that she didn't cry when her home fell into the river, and she didn't have sleepless nights over it because it was something monetary. But when some children came to her door with a special gift and told her their school had collected $100 for a flood victim and they had chosen her, she cried for the first time because of the kindness and love of the community. To me, this was a story of hope and love, a story of charity. (*Portraits of Loss, Stories of Hope*, published by Stories of Hope Volunteer Committee. 2005.)

BIBLIOGRAPHY

"Anasazi Diaspora," from *Navajo Visions and Voices Across the Mesa*, Shonto Begay, Scholastic Inc., New York: 1995

"Looter gets 37 months in prison in stolen artifacts case in Vegas." *The Las Vegas Sun Newspaper.* December 16, 2003.

"Nevada man, last of five sentenced in stolen relics case." *The Las Vegas Sun Newspaper.* January 19, 2004.

"Relic looters get prison." *The Las Vegas Sun Newspaper.* December 11, 2003.

"Stores of Hope Volunteer Committee." *Portraits of Loss, Stories of Hope* published by Portraits of Loss, Stories of Hope; St. George, Utah. 2005.

"Two more defendants in artifacts case to be sentenced." *The Las Vegas Sun Newspaper.* December 12, 2003.

ABOUT AUTHOR

Linda Weaver Clarke is from Color Country, which is located in southern Utah. It's a beautiful area full of red mountains, which sits like an oasis in the middle of the desert.

She is the mother of six daughters and has several grandchildren. Clarke is the author of several historical romances, a mystery/suspense series, cozy mystery series, and a children's book. All her books are family friendly. Visit www.lindaweaverclarke.com.

Made in the USA
Columbia, SC
05 September 2020